John Creasey – M:

Born in Surrey, England in 1908 in
were nine children, John Creasey gr   ......y
teller and international sensation. His more than 600 crime, mystery
and thriller titles have now sold 80 million copies in 25 languages.
These include many popular series such as *Gideon of Scotland Yard,
The Toff, Dr Palfrey* and *The Baron*.

Creasy wrote under many pseudonyms, explaining that booksellers
had complained he totally dominated the 'C' section in stores. They
included:

> *Gordon Ashe, M E Cooke, Norman Deane, Robert Caine Frazer,
> Patrick Gill, Michael Halliday, Charles Hogarth, Brian Hope, Colin
> Hughes, Kyle Hunt, Abel Mann, Peter Manton, J J Marric, Richard
> Martin, Rodney Mattheson, Anthony Morton* and *Jeremy York*.

Never one to sit still, Creasey had a strong social conscience, and
stood for Parliament several times, along with founding the One
Party Alliance which promoted the idea of government by a
coalition of the best minds from across the political spectrum.

He also founded the British Crime Writers' Association, which to
this day celebrates outstanding crime writing. The Mystery Writers
of America bestowed upon him the Edgar Award for best novel and
then in 1969 the ultimate Grand Master Award. John Creasey's
stories are as compelling today as ever.

THE TOFF SERIES

Here Comes the Toff

John Creasey

HOUSE OF
STRATUS

This edition published in 2012 by House of Stratus, an imprint of Stratus Books Ltd., Lisandra House, Fore Street, Looe, Cornwall, PL13 1AD, U.K.
www.houseofstratus.com

Typeset by House of Stratus.

A catalogue record for this book is available from the British Library and the Library of Congress.

ISBN 075513572-5
EAN 978-075513572-1

Chapter One

Of the Toff

There are so many stories of the Toff.

That gentleman, who is known socially as the Hon. Richard Rollison, to his friends as Rolly, and to a few disapproving relatives as Richard, will deny most of them, saying that they follow the lines of each other so closely that there is in fact only one story worth telling about him. Therein he is too modest – which is not one of his major faults – although it is probably true that he finds a monotonous similarity in the various adventures which have befallen him.

Mostly, he is the first to admit, these adventures are of his own choosing. In a really discursive mood he will go into the psychological reasons for his interest in crime, and present himself as a man of unusual moral awareness. He will even produce a somewhat startling and yet plausible argument to the effect that he was sent into this world as a squalling infant – or so the records say – that he might use the axe of retribution on many gentlemen whose illegal practices would otherwise have escaped their full punishment.

A man of many contradictions, the Hon. Richard Rollison.

Thus, with more money than he knew what to do with, he sometimes lived in positive luxury – while at others he lived so humbly that people who did not know him might have imagined that he could not boast two half-crowns. There were occasions when he delved deeply into the delights of the social whirl which takes possession of London two or three times a year. And there were other periods when all the charms of the Season, and the Season's lovelies, could not lure him from the East End, which he liked to call his spiritual home.

Of course, much that Rollison says must be taken with the proverbial pinch of salt. Few people know when the expression in his grey eyes is serious, few can tell when he is exerting himself to pull a leg sadly in need of pulling, and probably only Jolly – his man – knows when the Toff is worried.

Jolly himself is an example of the waywardness of the Toff – or, more accurately, of his reputation for waywardness. Many folk claim that Jolly's name is more likely to be Smith or Brown, but that his dyspeptic face, miserable as it always seems and is always likely to be, inspired the Toff to dub him Jolly. In point of fact, the rumour is not true, but the Toff likes to create the impression that it might be.

In selecting the stories of the Toff for presentation to a public that knows little of the man himself, one rule has to be followed. Anything which is unusual, anything which shows unexpected twists and turns – that alone qualifies a story for the telling according to the Toff, and he will allow nothing else to be written.

There is the story of the hobnailed boots.

The police gave it another name for their records, and the Press gave it various names for their headlines, but the Toff insists that the hobnailed boots were the key to the whole situation. Without them, he considered, it would have been humdrum and unworthy of recording.

He asks, with some justification, why a man should take his boots off during a London pea-souper, and whether any other case recorded at the Yard can show a hobnailed boot as Exhibit A, B or C? When the police (also with justification) point out that there was no such exhibit, he laughs – that quiet and yet rollicking laugh of his, wherewith the world seems a happier place – and claims that he cannot be responsible for their lack of perception.

It did not, of course, start with boots. Like quite a number of the Toff's adventures, it began in a fashionable restaurant in Mayfair – the Embassy, to wit – and at a time when the Toff was considering the blue eyes of a companion who was charming to look at and to talk to, who could dance, who could laugh, and who did not take life too seriously.

Her name was Anthea, which the Toff thought most pleasant-sounding, and her hair was fair, even golden, and her skin was blemishless. Her eyes had a starry light, and her lips were easy – and sometimes anxious – to kiss, although at the Embassy they were naturally redder than nature made them.

Anthea – Lady Anthea Munro – was Scottish, and very lovely.

There was nothing of the *jeune fille* about her, and although she knew of Rollison as the Toff, she had not once asked him to take her to the East End.

She danced with an effortless grace which made even the Toff forget that there were a hundred others dancing on the crowded floor of the Embassy on a night when outside it was cold, but inside over-warm. The hour – although Rollison did not know it at the time – was eleven-fourteen.

Anthea said: "You're a queer specimen, Rolly, aren't you?"

Rollison raised one eyebrow as he turned, while the strains of violins came sweet and haunting.

"I'm inclined to agree with you: queer is the word, up to a point. But I don't see why you should choose it."

"Try," said Anthea.

"Why?" asked Rollison. "You can tell me, and save me the trouble of thinking."

"Idiot." She smiled, her teeth glistening and very white. "Like you're real cool, you know."

"If the current mode is to prefix all statements with 'like', and say someone's 'real cool' in this hothouse," said Rollison, "I don't approve of it. And if this is a proposal, my sweet, be warned that I am a misogynist by the grace of God and the dreadful warnings of my married friends. Do we leave the subject?"

"No," said Anthea, "and it wasn't a proposal. I'm going to marry Jamie, a nice, stolid, wealthy, companionable, and interesting man who will make me perfectly happy."

"Lucky girl," said Rollison. "Does he know yet?"

3

"He only hopes," said Anthea. "I—oh, confound it, and there's an interval due."

The music had ended, and the crowd of well-dressed – even exclusively dressed – people made their way back to their seats. Rollison – as always – had contrived to secure a corner table, pleasantly cool, and yet not too close to others, and at a spot where service could be speeded up as he required it. A waiter, hovering, approached at the lift of his finger, and poured more champagne, replacing the bottle reverently on ice.

"Thanks," said Rollison, and as Anthea settled down in her chair, raised his glass. "To Jamie, when he hears the happy news."

"Fool," said Anthea again, but she drank laughingly. "Rolly, I think you're deliberately trying to make me drunk."

"Heaven forbid!" said the Toff with exaggerated horror. "There's nothing more repulsive than a pretty girl who's tipsy. Especially one so young."

Anthea lifted her hands, a quick gesture.

"There – you see. We've been here for two hours, and we had an hour together this afternoon, and that's the first time you've paid me a compliment. Even then it was back-handed."

"Oh," said the Toff, and sounded bereft of words – which was not the case, for he was a most talkative and self-possessed gentleman, and rarely stumped. As he expected, the single exclamation made Anthea go on.

"I don't think I've ever had the experience before. I've known men tongue-tied, but never one who could talk nineteen to the dozen without telling me the colour of my eyes."

Rollison's lips curved.

"I gave you credit for knowing that they're lovely." He lit a cigarette after she had refused. "I could have told you all about your eyes and hair, which is—I could have said—like spun gold. Or your teeth, normally to be compared with pearls. Or of lips which have been put to uses Jamie certainly would not approve, and which are distinctly kissable."

"I wonder," said Anthea a little dreamily, "whether Jamie will be able to kiss like you."

"In time, and with encouragement," said the Toff. "The right time, and—if I dare advise you—discreet encouragement I believe that on and immediately after engagements, dour young men suddenly wake up to the realization that there have been other lips, which thought, of course, enrages them. Surprising how many ingenuous young men there still are in existence. I ..."

"We are talking about you," said Anthea firmly. "Why aren't you like the rest? I've seen at least a dozen women ogling you tonight, and you've ignored them. And the dowdy ones, or the older ones, you smile at. Do you mean to do it, or is it accidental?"

Rollison laughed with real amusement.

"Anthea, you're a delight! I mean it, thanks be. The answer is that the old and dowdy who get little attention love it, and the young and beautiful who get plenty hate it. And if you will have it, my dear, I told you all that I think of your face and figure and voice and intelligence when I suggested that we might have fun together. I knew about Jamie, too, and that suggested you'd want to have your fling before he came down from Scotland. I'm surprised at you, though, you're taking a risk—he'll probably hear both about it and my dubious reputation."

"I can handle Jamie," said Anthea, with complete assurance. "And we're still talking about you. What makes you—well, look for crime?"

Rollison raised both brows.

"Do I?"

"Don't hedge!"

"That's not hedging, it's a question, and I'll answer it myself. I don't look for crime. I find it sometimes, but more often than not it finds me. I don't look for anything, sweetheart, but there are some things I come across that I don't particularly like and I try to prevent a repetition of them. Does that make sense?"

"More or less," said Anthea. "I ..."

She broke off, and the Toff's lips curved.

"Well done, Anthea. You just saved yourself from saying you'd like to tour the East End with me. Right?"

"Right. How *do* you know?"

"It must be the feminine streak in me," said Rollison. "It's obviously intuition, and as all women claim that only women have that, the feminine streak can be taken as read."

Anthea laughed.

Few would have suggested that there was anything feminine in Rollison. He stood more than seventy-two inches, was broad with it, and yet had a figure which delighted his tailor. He could be called handsome without stretching the word to cover any particular *mésalliance* of feature. His hair was dark and wavy. His jaw, which was square, had a prominence not out of proportion to his face, wherein the nose was straight and the lips well shaped. The wide-set eyes were grey, having the expression which sometimes suggests that a man is used to looking into long distances.

"All right, Rolly, it's the feminine streak in you. I knew it would be fatal if I asked."

Rollison's eyes gleamed.

"And now that you haven't asked, you hope that I'll be a perfect gentleman and offer?"

"We-ell," said Anthea, "Jamie comes back in two days' time, and I won't be free after that. But I'm not pressing you."

"No-o," said Rollison, and although the gleam remained in his eyes, she sensed that he was serious. "Anthea, the East End has many points I like but you wouldn't. Of course, it's vastly changed since the war, but too many of the old, bad streets survived to go on festering. Parts of it you'd call dirty and smelly. You'd think the people unspeakable, you'd consider the shops lousy, you would take one look at the river and think with nostalgia of Maidenhead. You'd dislike the smelly saloon bars and the smellier public bars, you'd find the children call after you, you'd get tired because you can't get a cab to take you from corner to corner, your shoes would be so thin that they'd wear through on the cobbles—yes, there are plenty of cobbled streets left, my sweet, don't imagine that Lancashire has a lien on them. You can't *look* at the East End. You've got to be part of it, and it takes years to get acclimatized. Be wise, and stay this side of Aldgate Pump."

Anthea said quietly: "It's fascinating, isn't it? I don't mean Chinatown, and all that nonsense—but the real people living there.

You're right, I know. I spent a week in Wapping, last year. I went to a boarding-house and paid thirty shillings a week for a room, and the first day I loved it. But" – she shrugged and smiled – "no one spoke to me, no one trusted me. I wanted to get to know them, but they drove me out in a week. Oh, they were polite, I don't mean they ignored me. But they remembered aitches too often, and the landlady always washed her hands before coming upstairs to my room. I felt a beast."

Rollison contemplated her for some minutes, and although the band started again, neither of them stood up. The smoke curled from the cigarette between his fingers, which were tanned a light brown, like his face. The champagne was bubbling slowly in their glasses, as if sullen and resentful at being ignored. And then Rollison said, without abruptness, but also without any apparent relation to what she had said: "Scotland's a grand walking country, Anthea."

She hesitated, and then averted her eyes. All enthusiasm had died out of her voice; she seemed deflated.

"Yes, isn't it?"

"No one who comes from there would be without a good stout pair of brogues, and a mac that doesn't look new, and a hat that the wind can blow off if it wants to. Jamie comes back in two days, my sweet, so that leaves us only tomorrow. I'll take you there, and we'll see whether the East End is more kindly towards you now."

Anthea's lips were parted, her eyes shining.

"Rolly, you—you darling!"

"I'm not a bit sure," said the Hon. Richard Rollison with a frown, "that you haven't been throwing histrionics to work me up to the offer."

"Couldn't we start tonight?"

"Strange though it may seem," said Rollison sardonically, "places of interest there close before midnight. Most people have to be up around six, to get to work by seven or eight. If they don't arrive on time they lose their job—and the vast majority like to work." He looked about him, and there was a twist to his lips which she had not seen before, an expression almost of disdain in his eyes. "Here are your won't-works, here are the real poor, even though they're rolling in money. There's hardly a man or woman here tonight who knows what real work is."

He stopped suddenly.

Anthea saw a strange transformation in him, saw disdain change to momentary surprise, and then to wariness.

She followed his gaze, and saw quite close to them an old man who was dancing with a woman in a black gown, a woman who was superbly beautiful, exotic, perhaps, with a feline grace which no one could fail to see. It was almost obscene to see her dancing with the grey-haired, tired-looking ancient.

The woman glanced at Rollison. Her expression hardened, obviously with surprise, and for a moment their eyes met. Then she turned her head, and a moment later she and her partner were hidden from sight.

Rollison drew a deep, slow breath.

Anthea said: "Rolly, what is it?"

"What is ...?" he broke off, and she knew that, for seconds past, he had not been aware of her presence. "A bit out of the past, Anthea."

"Not a pleasant bit?"

"No. I ..." he smiled, and again he lifted a finger for the waiter. "Did you see the woman in black?"

"Yes, of course."

"She is striking," admitted the Toff. "A very lovely lovely, is our Irma. Named Cardew, too, although I doubt if she admits it. Does Irma Cardew mean anything to you?"

Anthea stared. "No."

"The price of youth," said Rollison. "Three years ago she was acquitted of murder. She should not have been. Because where Irma goes there's trouble; often death, and certainly crime. I wonder who her victim is?"

"Victim?"

"The grey-head," said the Toff, and he was not smiling. "Rich and ready for the plucking, I fancy. Anthea, my precious, I'm going to take you home. If tomorrow is our day, tonight is mine, and I've found some work to do."

Chapter Two

Of Italian Art and Other Things

Had the Toff had his way, he would have gone from the Embassy without being noticed by the woman in the black gown. Nine people out of ten, with the same object in view, would have elected to leave via any one of the three emergency exits; but the Toff worked on the assumption that the woman called Irma would notice, in any case, that he had gone – and that she would guess he proposed to follow her.

He used the main doors, and waited for a moment or two in the foyer for Anthea to get her cloak. He was surprised that she kept him for so short a time, and looked down at her five feet two with a thoughtful expression.

"Have you discovered you're in a hurry?"

"Yes—because you won't want to waste time," said Anthea, and she seemed more serious – and unwittingly younger – than she had all the evening, except for that brief spell of disappointment when the Toff had misled her by introducing the quality of Scotland as a walking country.

"Very nicely thought," said Rollison, and his appreciation was sincere. "We'll be at your place in ten minutes."

"Are you going to follow her?" This as they squeezed through the same partition of the revolving doors to the street outside.

"I might even do that."

"Then just put me into a taxi."

"My dear girl …"

"Please, I don't want to crab you," said Anthea, and there was such obvious entreaty in her voice that the Toff shrugged and smiled, and pressed her arm.

"You're a nice child," he said.

"The only thing I won't forgive you is if you let me down tomorrow," she said quickly. "It's my last chance, remember."

"Tomorrow it shall be." He handed her into a cab, and told the driver to take her to Chamley Mansions, which were in Park Lane, and where her parents – who were excessively rich, a remarkable thing for a peer and peeress – had a flat. His last sight of her was as she leaned forward to look at him through the window, a street lamp shining on the diamond clip in her hair.

He waved – and turned towards Piccadilly.

Close by the Embassy, which he could watch from it, was a telephone kiosk. He slipped in, and dialled a Mayfair number.

After a short pause a deferential voice answered, a voice which could often be expressive, and which belonged to Jolly.

"Jolly …"

"Sir."

"Irma Cardew is back in London," announced the Toff, and he paused long enough for the information to sink in. Jolly's response was gratifying, because it consisted of utter silence. The Toff went on, casually to all appearances, and yet inwardly more concerned than he had admitted to Anthea. "She is at the Embassy, so get here quickly. If I'm not about, you will know that I've gone after her, but if I'm still here, you will follow. Having followed, you will wait until her companion either goes off alone, or goes into her flat—it will probably be a flat—with her. Is that clear?"

"Perfectly, sir. Three minutes, sir."

"Make it two," said the Toff, who usually invited impossibilities.

With characteristic thoroughness Jolly arrived in precisely three minutes, passing the Toff without acknowledging him. He thereby demonstrated his alertness, for as he passed, Irma and her companion came down the steps of the Embassy, and a commissionaire called a cab for them.

Jolly also secured one, twenty yards farther along the road. The Toff followed suit, and the three cabs moved off one after the other. Rollison wondered whether Irma would try to dodge him, and also wondered – with sardonic amusement – what reason she had advanced to her companion for this sudden departure.

He instructed his driver to follow Irma's cab.

It was not easy at night, and he was not sure of getting through. His doubts were vindicated, and Anthea would have been disappointed at what looked like a set-back. For at the first traffic lights in Piccadilly Irma's cabby made a quick burst of speed, and the Toff, with Jolly behind him, was held up.

The Toff kept on the road for three minutes, but saw no further signs of the cab and the woman he badly wanted to follow. He did not complain, even to himself, for he considered such indulgences a waste of time. He stopped his cab and climbed out, paying the man off as Jolly's cab drew up. The Toff joined his servant, and in silence they were driven back to the Toff's Gresham Terrace flat.

It was a remarkable flat in one way.

Except for the living-room, it was ordinary enough. Even that, but for one wall, was comfortable but not excessively so, suggesting good taste without ostentation. The exception, however, showed one of those bizarre and always unpredictable tendencies of the Toff.

It was covered – almost literally – with an assortment of weapons, and, as he liked to term them, trophies of the chase. There were knives by the dozen, and automatics, even old service revolvers, and three distinct kinds of pistols small enough to be held in the palm of the hand. There were blackjacks, small, shiny, leather-covered, and narrow bags containing lead shot, which induced unconsciousness with a minimum of injury in anyone they struck. There were sandbags, there were swords, there were daggers and krisses, there were ropes and cords, there were scarves – several of them brown-stained with dried blood – and there was even a small glass case, standing on brackets, which contained phials and bottles which were the actual containers of poisons which had been used in cases that had attracted the Toff's attention.

In London – both the East and the West Ends – there was much talk of the Toff's armoury, and of his Trophy Wall which was almost as legendary as the Toff himself. It amused him, he said, and it also caused Jolly much bother, for there were times when the Toff wanted to display a "piece" which Jolly considered was too large or else in excessive bad taste. Jolly usually had his way – although on occasions a particularly unattractive souvenir adorned the wall or the floor just beneath it for longer than he liked.

Into this room went the Toff and Jolly, who immediately stepped to a cocktail cabinet.

"Weak or strong, sir?"

"Neither," said the Toff, who had a reputation for drinking which was not wholly deserved. "I've had enough for the time being, Jolly, and the shock passed some time ago. Had you no idea that Irma was in London?"

"None at *all*, sir," said Jolly reproachfully. "I would have informed you immediately."

"Ye-es. Although I wouldn't put it past you to try to keep something up your sleeve. But I will overlook it this time! She is. She saw me. She wished she hadn't. She had a man with her."

"A young man, sir?" Jolly sounded almost deprecating as he broke a silence that had lingered for thirty seconds.

"Certainly not young, Jolly. It's no case of *joie de vivre*, or fun and games. Nor do I believe that Irma will ever sink to being kept by an octogenarian."

"It is hardly likely, sir." Jolly, standing at ease by the cocktail cabinet, and with the fingers and thumb of one hand pressed on the top, looked slight and grey and miserable. He had a face which most would have called nondescript, for he was rarely noticeable in a crowd. Nor were the features particularly good, being somewhat sharp, with the eyes deep-set and yet wide apart. "The man was over fifty, then, sir?"

The Toff looked at him sharply.

"I don't feel funny, Jolly. Irma back in London is the last thing I expected, and she's hooking the fellow for a certainty. As we can't find her at short notice, we'll have to try to find him. I've seen him about, but I can't place him."

"At a club, sir?"

"Quite likely at a club," admitted the Toff, and scowled. "Which means that I shall have to do a club-crawl tomorrow, Jolly, or—oh, damn!"

"Yes, sir?" Jolly was inquisitive.

"I'm busy tomorrow," said the Toff very thoughtfully, and he drew his forefinger along his nose, a trick he had, and of which he was unconscious. "I can't put the appointment off, that's certain. Irma will have to sweat for twenty-four hours."

"Quite likely she will, sir," murmured Jolly.

The Toff's eyes gleamed.

"I hope you're right! On the other hand, she appeared to be as calm as ever, and she got away from us nicely tonight. Too nicely. The boy friend, of course, could be involved in whatever racket she's playing, but I doubt that."

"You're sure there is a racket, sir?"

"I've told you," said the Toff, with dignity, "that Irma is in London. Irma would not be in London without some fell purpose. I—Jolly! A moment, Jolly, a single moment!"

He lifted a hand as if enjoining silence, and fingered the bridge of his nose, so obviously deep in thought that Jolly knew he had recalled where he had seen Irma Cardew's companion.

"Pictures," said the Toff, almost dreamily. "Paintings. Art. Art galleries. Italian paintings. A show of Italian art, Renaissance period, at the Balliol Gallery, Bruton Street. The name of one of the contributors, Jolly, one of the gentlemen who lent the pictures— Jolly, a catalogue of that show! In a hurry, if you please."

"Yes, sir," said Jolly. "It's in your room, sir."

It happened that the Toff had at one time been more than friendly with the Contessa Grinaldi, who – being Italian – had, of course, demanded to see the display of Italian art. The Contessa, who would have found it difficult to differentiate between a Picasso and an Annigoni, had voted herself delighted, and the catalogue would always remain one of her most treasured possessions. She had, of course, left it in the Toff's flat after her third and last visit, and Jolly – as was his habit – had stored it safely away. He brought it to the Toff.

There were a dozen pages devoted to the patrons of the Exhibition, and the fifth at which the Toff looked showed him a likeness of the man who had been with Irma Cardew. A likeness, that was, of a sort. The man seemed little more than fifty, and appeared more upright than the one he had seen that night. This suggested that the photograph was an old one, and touched up considerably, but it was enough for identification.

"Renway," said the Toff slowly. "Mr. Paul Renway, Jolly, whose kindness in supporting the exhibition is herein duly and suitably acknowledged. He owns ..."

Rollison stopped talking aloud, to read a long paragraph on the pictures which Renway owned, and which he kept in his London house. Disobligingly, the catalogue failed to give the address of that residence.

"But," said the Toff, putting the catalogue aside, "we're not going to worry about that, being owners of a telephone directory. You look up his address, Jolly, and go there quickly. Wait for an hour, or even two. If Irma comes out, follow her. If she doesn't, make what inquiries you can and if you can – but do nothing to arouse suspicions. Mr. Renway is a man with a reputation, and we should hate to spoil it."

"Of course, sir."

"While I," said the Toff, "will make myself pleasant at the Carlton Club. Waterer is a member there, and he haunts the place at night. He also owns Italian pictures, and he will doubtless give me the details of Renway's collection, with many a hint on the dishonesty of his methods of obtaining Masters which he, Waterer, would gladly steal. A troubled world, Jolly, and – what are you waiting for?"

"For you to finish, sir," said Jolly. He bowed and slipped out as the Toff sat back in an easy chair to consider the situation.

Nothing that occurred to him suggested that his estimate of Irma Cardew's return to London was erroneous. He remained surprised, for he had not thought it likely that she would show herself again for many years. The jury had acquitted her on the direction of a judge who had died soon afterwards. Although the Toff had wished the judge no harm, he was glad that, when Irma came up for trial again – as he believed she would – the same gentleman would not be in a position to help her escape.

For undoubtedly Irma had been guilty.

The police, including that gentleman who at once liked and detested the Toff – Chief Inspector McNab, to wit – knew all about Irma, knew that she had more than one murder to her discredit, and were aware of the most remarkable fact about her. She was that English rarity, a female gangster. The police and Rollison agreed on one point about her. The female of the species was more dangerous than the male.

Irma could, and would, kill – and even had killed – as remorselessly as any Chicago big-shot, and more readily than any gangster's moll. She was not a moll in the generally accepted sense of the word; her devotion to her brother, who had been killed in a gun fight with Rollison just before her arrest, had been one of several things to lift her out of the common rut.

She had a good mind, for another thing.

There had been times when the Toff had admired her, when he had known that had her moral make-up been different -and he was not thinking of her attitude towards sex – they could have been friends. But she possessed that something which had inspired a famous gentleman to coin the phrase, "an enemy of society."

Rollison had expected her to stay out of England.

He knew that she had left the country immediately after the trial, and his interest in her had been so great that he had gone to the trouble of finding out that for some months she had been in Hamburg, for several more she had stayed in Paris, and then – under various names – she had visited New York, Monte Carlo, Venice, Calcutta and the Cape. It suggested that on the reasonable fortune she had illegally garnered, she was seeing the world and having a good time. As there was nothing he could do to prevent it, the Toff had not complained.

Now, in London, she was a different proposition.

It seemed likely that her funds had run low, if they had not run out completely. That was one of the few things that would have brought her back. Another was a collaborator, for he doubted whether Irma would start anything entirely on her own.

Who, in London, was most likely to work with her?

Rollison could think of no one, for Master Crooks – he liked the capitals – were rare at all times, and just then, as far as he knew, completely non-existent.

The five minutes he had allotted for consideration being up, he donned his hat and coat again and went to the Carlton Club. By then it was well past midnight, but he was not surprised to find Sir Matthew Waterer, an old-middle-aged gentleman of considerable wealth, sitting in his favourite corner of the smoking-room, and holding forth – to the annoyance of most of his companions. Waterer was at that moment on his third favourite hobby-horse – the degeneracy of modern youth. It took Rollison five minutes to break in on his conversation – and thus earn the silent acclaim of a half circle of unwilling listeners – and another five to corner Waterer, and discuss his first favourite hobby-horse – Art.

The Toff, a patient man, had eight minutes of Art before he led the conversation to Renway. Immediately he gathered that Waterer disliked Renway, and assumed that Renway's collection of Italian paintings was superior to Waterer's. It was. If the latter gentleman was to be believed, however, not a single item of Renway's collection had been honestly come by. Rollison was silent for some moments in sheer admiration of a man who could so ruthlessly discard all common decency about a fellow-collector, and who held the laws of slander in such obvious contempt. Nevertheless, he had a clear picture of Renway in his mind.

A rich man – a man of few friends – a man with a nephew likely to inherit most of his fortune. A big-business man who did not know that it was past time he retired. A misogynist – Waterer rolled the word out with obvious enjoyment, and the Toff smiled, as he remembered using it on himself when he had been talking to Anthea – and yet a man who was thinking of getting married. Rumour had it that he was engaged.

The Toff raised a metaphorical eyebrow.

Waterer was short, florid, grey-haired, with a veined nose and a thick, rasping voice. He waved his right hand as he talked, and kept the other in his pocket. He fixed the Toff with protuberant, fish-like eyes.

"Yes, Rollison, at his age. Obscene, I consider it. Marriage is a thing for the young, and …"

"And who," asked Rollison gently, "is the lucky lady?"

"A woman named Curtis, I'm told. Haven't thought much about it." Waterer then proceeded to prove that he had made every inquiry possible short of a personal approach to Renway, and further described the lady as no better than a *demi-mondaine*. He did not use the word, but something far more crude. He admitted – not without a suggestion of lasciviousness – that she was good to look at, and his description of her fitted Irma Cardew.

Which suggested that Irma was either (a) seriously contemplating marriage, or (b) planning a large-scale fraud on the millionaire. The latter was the more likely.

It was nearly one o'clock when Rollison got home, to find Jolly waiting for him, with a report.

Jolly had reached the millionaire's St. John's Wood house ten minutes before Irma had come out, to be driven away by Renway's chauffeur. She had entered a flat near Park Lane, which spoke of money; discreet inquiries of the night porter had elicited the fact that she had been there for some weeks, that she was next door to a man named Kohn, and that she had a habit of staying at Kohn's flat at hours which were not considered proper.

And thus the Toff became interested in the man named Kohn, but not as interested as he would have been had he known a little more of Kohn's past life.

For Kohn was not an honest man.

Chapter Three

Anthea's Day Out

Had there been no Jolly, Anthea would doubtless have been disappointed.

Which does not suggest that she was enamoured of Jolly, for, in fact, she considered him a vaguely interesting freak, and could not understand why the Toff bore with him. The Toff saw no reason to enlighten her on Jolly's usefulness, nor on the fact that he was one of the most astute men in London, that he had a flair for finding the flaws in the Toff's arguments – which was what the Toff wanted while theorizing on crime – and that he was familiar with the East End, the West End, the suburbs and even Greater London. Moreover, he was attached to him.

Rollison, however, was able to delegate certain important items concerning Renway and Irma to Jolly, and thus was free to spend the promised day with Anthea. He called for her at her parents' flat, to find his lordship out and her ladyship a little dubious about her daughter's friendship with the Hon. Richard Rollison.

In the course of a three-minute conversation the majestic and full-breasted woman who was Anthea's mother mentioned Jamie seven times, and as the Toff stood up on Anthea's arrival, he said, *sotto voce*:

"Believe me, Lady Munro, Anthea is safer with me than with Jamie. I shall deliver her back intact."

"What," demanded Anthea, as a footman closed the front door behind them, "did you say to mother? I've never seen her so flabbergasted in her life."

Rollison crooked an eyebrow.

"I was warning her against Jamie, darling."

"What?" Anthea was amused, yet puzzled.

"To divert her base suspicions from my own innocent head," said Rollison. "Now let me look at you." In the middle of Park Lane he stood and held Anthea at arms' length, seeing the soiled mackintosh, the stout and worn brogues, the shapeless hat. "You'll do," he approved. "You may not look one of us to the gentlemen we're visiting, but certainly you won't look one of the nobs. At first glance, that is. You've a something, Anthea, which won't stay hid."

"Thank you, sir. Where do we go first?"

"By bus to Aldgate Pump, and then we walk."

"Good. I—but just a moment!" Anthea stopped, and held the Toff at arms' length, scowling. "*You're* dressed to kill."

"The Toff always is," said Rollison, cheerfully. "They'd be disappointed if he wasn't. Have you seen one of these?"

"These" were several visiting cards which, when they were on the bus, she examined with some care. They said quite simply that the Hon. Richard Rollison lived at Gresham Terrace, and was a member of the Carilon Club.

"What about them?"

"Turn over," said Rollison.

On the reverse side of the cards were several pencil sketches, and Anthea started. She saw a top hat set at a rakish angle, a swagger cane, and a monocle, the string hanging down and tied at the end to the cane. They were absurd little drawings, and yet they conveyed the name perfectly.

The Toff ...

"You are a fool! Why do you use them?"

"To frighten people," said Rollison.

"I don't believe it."

"Which doesn't mean it's not true. Those cards," added the Toff somewhat self-consciously, half wishing that he had not brought them into display, "have an effect not unlike a grenade when put through the letter-box at the right moment. Which is quite enough of me – we're sight-seeing, remember."

He took her to Wapping and the Hundred Arches; he took her to the Pool, and the hundreds of little alleyways leading from it. He showed her quaysides where murder had been committed; he showed her the bearded boatman who found bodies in the river frequently, and called them "deados", and took them always to the Surrey side, because from the authorities there he received more payment than if he kept them on the Middlesex side. He showed her public houses which were the rendezvous of crooks, he pointed out pick-pockets, even one convicted murderer recently out after serving eleven years of a "life" sentence.

He led her through dingy, narrow streets where women foregathered at the front doors and talked and shouted, laughed and swore, with babies at their breasts as often as not – or so it seemed to Anthea. They passed the great post-war blocks of flats, tatty with washing drying on balconies, bleak in their tarmac surrounds. They saw whole districts where most of the occupants were hard-working citizens, where every member of every family contributed something to the family exchequer, and yet – because of high prices, and hire-purchase commitments – failed to have quite enough.

He showed her the Indian and Jamaican quarters, many still undeveloped, overgrown bombed lots, ruined houses, yet undemolished, notoriously used by the cheap prostitutes now run off the streets. He took her through an empty hovel which had once been a coiner's den, and showed her the relics of a broken plaster cast from which half-crowns and florins had been made.

She said very little, but she listened, and her eyes were bright with interest.

She was astonished by one thing.

Everywhere people seemed to know the Toff. He was smiled at, waved to, and talked to a dozen times. He had a pocketful of coppers and dispensed them among the smaller children, never making one jealous against another. There were, it was true, people who kept stoney-faced when he passed, others who swore: they were gentlemen, he assured her, who would gladly put a knife in his back.

He pointed out a gross, pot-bellied man with a scar on his right cheek, whose hair was cropped close, and whose discoloured teeth showed in a snarl as they passed.

Anthea, for the first time, looked perturbed.

"Ugh, what a brute! Who was he?"

"That's Dinger," said the Toff off-handedly. "He's just come out after a sentence for bigamy."

"Bigamy—that creature?"

"You haven't seen his wives," said the Toff, and then, as casually: "He handled dope, too, and that was where we quarrelled. I was never able to pin it on to him, but that scar on his cheek was from my knife. We had a scrap in the dark; he wore knuckle-dusters and used a razor."

Anthea shivered.

"Rolly—it's terribly dangerous. Why do you?"

"I don't quite know," said the Toff, and that was the whole truth. "My dear, I'm getting hungry, and so are you. Shall we eat?"

She nodded, still thinking of Dinger, and the fight by night which Rollison had dismissed in a few words, but which had conjured up visions likely to keep her company at night.

She had wanted to see the East End, and he was showing it to her. Her reactions were better than he had anticipated, and yet he wondered whether a whole day would not be too long.

In a street near the Mile End Road he turned into a coffee shop. The benches – where half-a-dozen stevedores and several labourers and two slatternly women sat – were hard, with high backs separating one cubicle from the next. The bill of fare was chalked up on a slate hanging on the wall, thus:

Joint & 2 veg.	3 / 3d.
Pudding – 5d.	Tea – 6d.
Steak & Kid.	3 / 6d.
Sausage & Mash – (1) 1 / 11d. (2) 2 / 3d.	

A girl in a dirty apron, who looked no more than fourteen, waited for their order. Her greasy auburn hair could have been a delight, but was hanging in neglected strands. Coarse, friendly shouts hailed her from the benches.

"Come orn, Gert!"

"Watcher waitin' for—yer pension?"

"Never mind, 'Andsome, gimme me sawsidge."

Anthea gave it up.

"Steak and kidney pudding twice, with vegetables," ordered Rollison to Gert, and the girl flounced off, returning more quickly than seemed possible with two steaming platefuls.

"Good stuff," said the Toff, his eyes gleaming. "Try it."

It was good stuff, although the suet roll which followed was too sickly for Anthea, and the tea that came afterwards was thick and black and sugary. But there was a fascination for her about the coffee shop, the girl who looked so unkempt and young and yet exchanged backchat with the wit of a woman twice her age.

As the Toff started to get up, he paused, for a man in a spotlessly white apron, with a large flabby face and a long black moustache, came out from the kitchen.

"I thought it was you," he said, and his hand went out for the Toff to grip. "'Ow's tricks, Mr. R? Not on the look-abaht, I 'ope."

"Not at your shop, Sam, you're always reliable."

Sam sniffed, eyeing Anthea curiously.

"Maybe, maybe not, Mr. R. Gits some rum customers 'ere sometimes. You 'eard anything?"

"No," said the Toff.

"Irma's aht," said Sam, in so low a voice that Anthea could not catch the words.

The Toff said gently: "Yes, I had heard that. Do you know where she is?"

"I bin wonderin'," said Sam. "Charlie Wray's the most likely fer 'er to visit, I reckon, 'e useter work fer 'er brother. If you 'as a smack at 'er, smack 'er 'ard, Mr. R. She ain't up to no good."

"We think as one," said the Toff. "I'll let you know if anything develops, Sam. Meanwhile, meet Miss Munro."

Sam turned his long black moustache in the direction of Anthea, and with care wiped his hand on the inside of his apron before offering it to her. His grip was surprisingly firm. As he smiled she saw the roguish expression in his eyes, and realized for the first time that there was something attractive about him.

"*How* de do?" asked Sam, with considerable emphasis on the "H". "*H*everything as yer liked it?"

"It was excellent," said Anthea.

"That's the ticket. Sam's fer food wot fills yer, that's my motter." He offered his hand again, even attempted something of a bow, and saw them to the door. As they went out of earshot, Anthea said: "There you are, you see. I *must* look a freak to them, Rolly."

"Darling, those eyes of yours do it, and your voice. But don't worry about that, with Sam it was a sign of respect extended to all those whom I bring with me. It's a whispering shop."

"A what?"

"A whispering shop. If anything's happening that the police don't know and want to, they try Sam's. He's not a squealer—a police informer—but if there's any really nasty stuff about he will whisper. Most of these people will give drug-traffickers away discreetly, and there aren't many who like the black."

"The black what?"

"Oh, such innocence!" exclaimed the Toff, and squeezed her arm. "Blackmail, darling. The extorting of money by threats of the disclosure of unhappy incidents from a man or woman's past, or the unbaring of a skeleton in a reputable family's cupboard."

"Thank you," said Anthea coldly. "What was he talking to you about?"

"The woman in black whom we saw last night."

Anthea whistled.

"Does it get round like that?"

"It does," said Rollison. "Everything reaches the East End in time, and usually quick time. There are more knowledgeable people here than you wot of. And now, look at that pub on the corner."

It was a dingy looking place with the woodwork green painted, but not recently, and many chalk marks along it, including a hammer and sickle, and, close by, both the lightning-streak-in-a-circle sign of British Fascism, and the not unsimilar cipher of "Ban the Bomb". The windows of the pub were dirty, the doorstep wanted cleaning, and one glass panel was boarded up. The boards were new.

"A recent rough house at the Blue Dog," said Rollison, and for the first time Anthea noticed a small hanging sign with a picture of a small terrier painted in blue.

"What kind of a place is it?"

"Incredibly low," said Rollison, and Anthea fancied that he was not as carefree as he had been earlier in the day. He walked slowly past the Blue Dog as if he hoped someone would come out or go in.

Someone did.

A youngish man, with outmoded winkle-picker shoes and clothes of flashy cut, pushed open the swing doors of the saloon bar, and swaggered on to the pavement. As he stood there, another man came from the pub, a vast creature, so fat that it seemed impossible for him to get through the door. He was in shirtsleeves, and wearing a green baize apron.

"Sure, Sidey, sure, you'll git yer whack, don't you worry. 'E never ..."

And then Anthea saw the expression on the fat man's face freeze, and he looked towards the Toff. Rollison appeared not to notice him, but Anthea was conscious of a shock, conscious of the fact that the sight of the Toff had affected the fat man in a way which seemed volcanic.

The flashily dressed one snapped: "'E'd better not come it, Charlie, I ..."

And then he, too, saw the Toff.

Exactly the same thing happened. Furtive, thin and unpleasant features stiffened, and for a moment his mouth stayed open. And then he straightened his shoulders, and muttered something that Anthea did not catch. He marched off down the street without another word to Charlie, who turned into the Blue Dog with the door banging heavily behind him.

Anthea said:

"Rolly, they were scared of you."

"Ye-es," said the Toff, "and not entirely without reason, my dear. When two men look at me like that they've got heavy burdens on their consciences. Yes, things are moving, and in a way I'm not sorry."

"Moving to what?"

"If I knew, they'd stop moving," said the Toff. "One of the difficulties of dealing with bad men is that you don't know just what the bad men are being bad about. The gentleman in mauve is named Sidey, I think. Charlie Wray owns the pub, and it's one of the worst in London." He smiled down at her, and there was in his expression a rollicking, devil-may-care insouciance which forced her to smile back. "Our next point of interest, lady, is a low dive frequented mostly by Chinatown. Don't laugh at Limehouse, my dear, Limehouse is not laughable—even under the Welfare State."

Anthea, a little later, agreed.

By then it was half-past three, and the Toff was wondering whether to make a day of it. Anthea, however, seemed the reverse of tired, and he wanted her to enjoy herself to the uttermost. It was with this generous thought in mind that he started to cross a cobbled road: and a car swept into it.

An old Morris, so battered that it was barely recognizable, and yet it was travelling fast. Anthea stopped in the middle of the road, caught in two minds. The Morris came straight on, and then Anthea felt herself lifted off her feet, found herself in the Toff's arms – and actually sailing through the air.

For the Toff jumped.

He jumped just in time, and the Morris rattled past, the red-faced driver leaning out of his window to swear at them. Anthea was pale as she stood on her own – and then she winced, and would have fallen had the Toff not saved her.

"Trouble?" asked Rollison quickly.

"My—ankle, I think. I ricked it." She kept most of her weight on one foot, and looked at him squarely. "Rolly, was that an accident?"

"Of course, it …"

"*Was* it …"

The Toff's eyes narrowed a little as he said: "I can't be sure, Anthea. The driver was a friend of Charlie Wray's, and Charlie was annoyed that I saw him talking with Sidey. On the other hand, the driver swore at us, which suggests he was as scared as we were."

"I—see."

"But he might have put the scare on for my benefit," admitted the Toff, who had not turned a hair. "I'm sorry about this ankle, Anthea. Will it carry you, do you think, or shall I?"

She tried it out gingerly, and then shook her head.

"There isn't a chance."

"Too bad," said Rollison. "I'll get you into the Mile End Road, there's a better chance of getting a cab there."

He lifted her bodily, and in three minutes they were in the Mile End Road, being stared at by numerous passers-by. A taxi was standing at a rank, and Rollison beckoned it. He directed the man to Anthea's flat, and while they were in the cab they were silent for a while. Then Anthea said: "Do you think they tried to kill you?"

"It could be. Don't brood over it, Anthea, it's happened before."

"It might succeed some day."

"We all have to die," said the Toff. "Taken by and large, have you enjoyed yourself?"

"I—don't—know," said Anthea frankly. "I wouldn't have missed it for the world, but the way that fat man looked at you, and then—oh, well," she added, and her eyes shone, "you ought to be able to look after yourself."

"I'll try! I wish your day hadn't been spoiled by a fat man and a swollen ankle," went on the Toff, "but you've seen plenty, and you'll be off your feet for a few days, to Jamie's great disappointment."

But Anthea didn't think about Jamie.

She pondered over the Toff, and the strange mixture that went to the making of him. He could take an evening at the Embassy and a day in the East End with the same aplomb, and he seemed to have as many friends in the one neighbourhood as the other. There was danger for him, and she felt it intuitively and knew that he was aware of it. She believed that he was preparing to do battle again, and she thought with a shudder of the fat man and the Morris which had so nearly run him down.

She was thinking of them that night, when the Toff again visited the East End, but not as he had been during the day. It is unlikely that she would have recognized him, but she would have noticed the new boards across a door panel of the pub which attracted his custom.

And for him she would have been afraid.

Chapter Four

Developments in a Fog

Jake Benson wiped the back of his hand across his mouth, banged his glass down, and winked at Charlie Wray, the owner of the Blue Dog in Wapping. Benson was short and thick-set, but lopsided. He drooped a little on the right, while the right side of his face was lower than the left, giving him a particularly villainous expression and a perpetual grin.

"O.K., Charlie boy! Now I'm orf to do a job o' work; but I'll be seeing yer."

"Don't forgit to do it proper; and use a knife—it's quiet," wheezed Charlie Wray.

Obviously he thought he had cracked a joke of the first quality, for he cackled and was still wheezing with merriment when Benson reached the swing-doors. Charlie was a vast man – as Anthea knew – twenty stone if he was a pound, a quivering jelly of a fellow whose bland face deceived some people into thinking he was the soul of benevolence. A man who looked fully into his little brown eyes would have been disabused very quickly, for Charlie Wray, although superficially honest – which meant that he had never been caught in any crime by the police – certainly was not a nice man.

Nor was Jake Benson.

They were two of a kind, dissimilar though they were in appearance. Benson's face was tanned a deep mahogany, and his skin was like hide; Wray's was white and dimply, and usually streaked with sweat.

Benson's crimes had been committed, for the most part, on the high seas, and he, too, had succeeded in creating what a defending solicitor would have called an unblemished reputation.

This job for "Mr. Brown" would mar it if he were foolish enough to make a mistake.

As Benson opened the door another man reached it. Whether he had not seen Benson, or whether he was deliberately trying to get out of the pub first, no one knew, but it remained a fact that they collided. The stranger – a stranger to the Blue Dog, although a denizen of Wapping, if his soiled clothes and muffler and peaked cap were tokens – drew back a pace, muttering an apology.

"I'm sorry, mister ..."

"I should ruddy well think you are!" snarled Benson, whose toes had suffered. "Git aht of my way before I bash yer face in."

He caught the man by the shoulder, sent him reeling back into the Blue Dog, and without another glance at him went out into the night. For a moment his footsteps echoed back into the pub, then faded out. The half-dozen loungers remaining there regarded the offender with some curiosity.

He was standing a couple of yards from the door, looking at it fixedly, with his shoulders hunched and his fists clenched. No one could see his face clearly, for his peaked cap was pulled low over his eyes, a habit by no means uncommon.

"Come on, buddy!" called Charlie Wray, in his oiliest voice. "Don't you be worrying erbaht Jake. 'E never meant nothing – take it from me. 'Ave one on the 'ouse."

It was a gesture that surprised the regular patrons of the Blue Dog, for Charlie was notoriously mean. But it did not impress the stranger, who snarled something unprintable under his breath, and barged out of the pub.

The fog outside grew thicker as Benson neared the river, and his footsteps were muffled; suddenly they stopped altogether. He was at the entrance of a narrow cul-de-sac that led to the warehouses facing the river, and he knew that no one was likely to be passing.

His actions then might have interested any policeman – or, for that matter, any citizen – for he took off his heavy boots. He put them with some care against the wall and padded on, making no sound at all. His feet were hardened by years of standing on ships' decks and frequent soaking in brine.

No light broke the darkness; occasionally the muffled wail of a ship's siren disturbed the stillness of the night. Here the fog was even thicker, and Benson's grin was twisted more than usual, for this was just what he wanted. No ships at the wharves could be loaded in the pea-souper, and the occasional watchman, who might have noticed him, would be blinded by the fog.

It was a perfect night for murder.

Only a man who knew the district like the palm of his hand could have gone on with so little hesitation. Apart from the quietness of his movements, the crook was making no attempt to conceal himself; he did not listen for approaching footsteps, and once when a man passed him he made no effort to move out of the way.

Not once did he appear to realize that the man he had struck at the Blue Dog had followed him, for that man's feet were shod as carefully as Benson's, if with greater comfort, for he wore rubber soles. At no point was there more than twenty yards separating them, and if Benson blessed the fog, so did his pursuer.

They were nearing the river. The lapping of the water against the sides of small boats and against the wharf walls came clearly. The creaking of ropes and hawsers murmured through the silence, but nothing could be seen through the all-enveloping fog.

Benson went slowly and more furtively as he neared the edge of the wharf. He took a small torch from his pocket, and the pencil of light stabbed through the gloom. It curled eerily in and out until it lit on a stanchion; Benson moved across to it and sat down, making the perch as comfortable as possible. A match scratched against the side of a box and flared up as Benson lighted a small cigar, the end of which glowed red a few inches from his nose, but without illuminating his features.

The man who had followed him could see the glow, but nothing else. He waited motionless, and for all the noise he made he might not have been there.

Ten minutes passed, and at last Benson stirred, taking a quick turn across the wharf. He was listening acutely now for an expected sound, and he shone the light of his torch on his watch to see that it was twenty minutes past nine. The man he was to meet was five minutes late.

"Blast 'im," Benson muttered aloud. "I'll teach the swab to keep me waitin'."

A moment later he chuckled, an unpleasant sound that fell on the ears of the watcher. The chuckle lasted for several seconds, for Benson was a specialist at appreciating his own jokes. He would teach his man, all right, and …

Heels sounded on the flagstones abruptly.

Benson stood up again as the approaching footsteps grew nearer, and another pencil of light stabbed a few yards through the fog. Benson raised his voice cautiously, turning towards the light.

"That you, Sidey?"

"That's me." The torch went out, and the silent listener repeated the name to himself several times, to make sure he did not forget it, while Sidey went on: "What a perishing blurry night to bring me out, Benson."

"Shut yer trap!" growled Benson. "You'll have a dozen blinkin' dicks along here in a minute."

"What a hope, on a night like this!" The man named Sidey gave a hoarse gasp of merriment, and the sound came ghostily through the darkness. "Well, I've come to collect. Where's the cash?"

"I've got it," grunted Benson. "Come 'ere."

They were close enough to see each other now, although Benson was holding something in his right hand which the other man did not see. He was expecting payment for services rendered, and despite the filthy night he was looking forward to a holiday on the strength of it.

A long holiday …

Benson's left hand stretched out suddenly, and gripped the other's arm. There was something frightening in the steel-like grip, and the man tried to draw back, his voice rising in alarm, but Benson's grip was too powerful.

"What the hell are you doin'?"

"Shut up, you fool!" snarled Benson. "Listen, Sidey, you tried to be clever once too often, see? You won't do it again. You're gettin' yours – and it's comin' now!"

There was time only for a half-scream to come from the man's lips; it stopped suddenly, ending in a choking, sickening gurgle. There was a sudden, shivering pain at his neck that lasted for a split second, and then, as Benson withdrew his support, the man's body slumped down to the ground.

The silent watcher, who could see no more than vague shapes in the fog, went taut; and then, as he realized that he could do nothing, he relaxed and continued waiting.

"An' *that's* what you've collected." Benson muttered the words under his breath as he knelt down, to make sure the man was dead. Then he took a handkerchief from his pocket and carefully wiped the handle of the knife to clean it of prints. He dropped the weapon on the man's body, and, less than a minute after the murder, turned away and moved silently into the darkness.

For a few minutes something akin to panic filled him but as he put distance between himself and the body his confidence returned. By the time he reached the *cul-de-sac* where he had left his boots, he was prepared to do the same thing again, provided "Mr. Brown" paid as well.

And then he had a shock, and the panic returned a hundredfold. It was frightening, unreasoning, making him feel cold and clammy, and yet hot.

For his boots were gone.

He made sure, searching along the wall and shivering all the time, and then he turned and almost ran in the direction of the Blue Dog. The man who had shadowed him followed, and Benson's fear would have turned to undiluted terror had he seen the expression on the man's face.

Charlie Wray was in the private room on top of the public bar when Benson returned. A single glance at the seaman's face told him of trouble, and he half-rose out of the chair into which his gross body was squeezed.

"What have you bin doin'?"

"Git me a drink!" gasped Benson.

He dropped into a seat, and his hands were trembling. Charlie's eyes narrowed as he waddled across to a cupboard. In a few seconds Benson was gulping a neat whisky, and the spirit revived his courage, even making him think he had acted like a fool. Charlie Wray listened to his story, a derisive smile on his lips.

"So because some nit pinched the boots he fell over," he said acidly, "you get the blasted heebies! That ain't the kind o' show we want from you, Benson, and the sooner you know it, the better. We want nerve, see?"

Benson finished a second tot of whisky, and glared ill-temperedly into Charlie's eyes, Dutch courage gathering within him.

"I can do my part with anyone. Sidey's gone, see, clean as a whistle. Don't you come any of that wif me, Charlie!"

"*I* won't start it," said the fat pubkeeper, with emphasis on the "I". "But someone else might."

"Who's goin' ter tell him?" Benson looked murderous.

"Nar then!" said Charlie, bland in a moment. "I'm not, an' you know it. But someone else might a' seen you rush in, Jake, and you never know who's working fer the Boss. Still, it's a foggy night, and yer luck's in. Forgit it, son, forgit it."

As he finished speaking he reached for the telephone near him. Benson, breathing more easily, was now inclined to be bellicose. He glared at Charlie as the latter said wheezily into the mike: "Mr. Brown, please."

The man at the other end of the wire said: "Speaking."

Benson knew him only as Brown, but Charhe Wray knew him as a Mr. Leopold Kohn, and had often worked for the man in the past. Charlie, in fact, was a go-between, who took no direct part in any crimes; he was too valuable as a giver-and-taker of vital messages, a hider of men and contraband, to be laid open to police action.

Kohn's voice was cold.

"What is it tonight, Wray?"

"Benson's in, sir. The job's O.K."

"No trouble at all?"

"Not so's I know, sir.' Charlie winked at Benson as he spoke, and omitted to mention the matter of the lost boots.

Kohn grunted: "Good. Tell Benson to report to me at Highgate at ten o'clock tomorrow morning, and tell him to be on time."

"Ten o'clock tomorrer, sir, on the pip. Right, Mr. Brown. That's O.K."

The man at the other end rang off without the formality of a goodbye, but Charlie's face was wreathed in smiles, as if all was right with the world.

"There y'are, Jake. You'll report and collect the dough tomorrer, easy as kiss me. I—*Wot* the hell!"

He broke off as a sound came at the door – or what seemed at the door. Benson heard it, too, but Benson was slower to move than Charlie Wray. The pubkeeper shifted his great bulk like lightning, and had the door open in a trice.

The landing outside was well lighted, but he saw nothing, and he turned back a moment later, muttering to himself, while below stairs, just out of sight, a stranger stood motionless.

"Could 'a swore I heard somethin'. It must 'a bin you putting the wind up me, Jake. Well, that's O.K., then, all hunky-dorey."

"I'll doss here tonight," said Benson.

"Welcome as the flowers, Jake, my word on it. I'd better be going downstairs, or they'll be givin' free drinks."

A free drink at the Blue Dog was certainly a rarity, and Benson laughed appreciatively, while Charlie eased himself down the stairs and into the bar. The only thing he saw worth noticing was that the man against whom Benson had banged earlier in the evening had come back for another drink. But the stranger was as surly and morose as he had been before, and his eyes – which Charlie might have recognized – were still covered by the peak of his cap. Charlie did not try to encourage him in conversation, but he might have done had he known that the surly one could have laid his hands on Benson's boots.

"So Sidey's gone," said Irma, known as Curtis, but whose real name was Cardew. "Why?"

Mr. Leopold Kohn, sitting at a large desk with the light shining down on his almost bald pate, nodded and smiled – unpleasantly. After a fashion, he was a handsome, even a distinguished-looking man, and dressed immaculately. So was his companion, although the unrelieved black of her dress would have struck some people as an affectation rather than mourning. None the less, it suited her.

There was a pantherish beauty about Irma that the sombre lack of colour did nothing to destroy, and the close-fitting lines of her gown seemed to emphasize the almost animal perfection of her figure. Her eyes, lips, and cheeks held colour, however, the former blue but cold, lips which were naturally well-shaped, outlined in scarlet, cheeks rouged enough, but not too much.

"Yes, he's gone," said Kohn. "Sidey knew just a little too much, my dear. Among other things, he knew that Martin had been working for us on the old man's accounts." Kohn smiled mirthlessly. "And on the strength of that, Sidey asked for more money, threatening to discuss his knowledge elsewhere if he didn't get it."

"You're a callous devil," said Irma slowly.

"There are times," said Kohn, with that same mirthless smile, "when I would not call you kind, my dear, although at other times perhaps you are. However, I am also careful. Benson, who so obligingly expunged Sidey for us, knows me only as Mr. Brown."

Irma's eyes were narrowed.

"I've never had much faith in disguises," she said, "but yours is good, I will say that. How do you manage it?"

"By being simple." Kohn shrugged his shoulders, but was obviously pleased. "Tinted glasses, cheek pads to fatten my face, different clothes, and a padded stomach—nothing more, my dear. But we were talking about Sidey. He was killed by a sixpenny bread-knife, wiped clear of fingerprints, and the Fates even sent a fog to help us. He is a known crook, and the police will put it down to a thieves' quarrel, and assume that there is not much chance of finding their man. I do not make any mistakes, Irma, and you can take it from me that Sidey had to go."

Irma shrugged gleaming white shoulders which her black dress emphasized, made even more seductive. She looked almost bored by the quick but pedantic voice of the speaker.

"All right. But be careful, Leo."

"My dear, I was born and bred to affairs like this, and I ..."

He broke off, for the woman interrupted him. There was a concentrated fury in her voice that astonished him, a cold savagery in her eyes which seemed to come without any cause.

"So was I—and so was Bram. And he died."

"Of course," said Kohn. "Of course, my dear, forgive me."

He looked as uncomfortable as he was ever likely to, for the death of Irma Cardew's brother had become what he privately called a bee in her bonnet. For his part, he was glad for several reasons that Bram Cardew had been killed. He was glad, too, that Irma now called herself Curtis; it seemed so much safer.

In a dozen world capitals, and over many years, Leopold Kohn and Bram Cardew had specialized in crimes out of the ordinary. It had mattered little what they were, provided the stakes were high. Cardew, who had always worked with his sister, had shown Kohn a clean pair of heels on several occasions, and Kohn had resented it, without showing his resentment.

It was before Kohn came to this country that the Cardews, as a team, met their Waterloo. In an affair that concerned the carrying of arms and ammunition to a foreign power, they found Rollison on their trail. Rollison, known so colloquially as the Toff, had followed it relentlessly until Bram Cardew was killed and his sister stood trial for murder; for it was the Toff's way to succeed and, as he would say bitterly, the law's job to turn success bitter, since Irma was acquitted on lack of evidence, at the prompting of that now deceased judge.

For some years she had done nothing, and since Bram's death she had worn unrelieved black. Her love for her brother had been the guiding factor in her life, even the Toff had admitted that.

Kohn had met her again at Monte Carlo, and, after a decent interval from her trial, had asked her to join him. She was both clever and attractive, and she knew the tricks of the trade. She would, he had believed, prove a perfect partner; and in some ways she had, particularly in the operations abroad. Only on one point was Kohn unable to move her. He had remonstrated with her black dress – which she left off only when she was "on duty" – and the reply had inevitably been the same.

"To remind me of Bram, Leo." Her lips would twist oddly, and her eyes would stare into Kohn's. "I'll wear it until I've got Rollison."

After a few efforts Kohn had given up the struggle. Her hatred of Rollison he considered absurd, for he knew very little of the man, and was inclined to think she overrated his ability and his potential menace. When he suggested as much, Irma would smile at him obscurely and tell him to thank his Fates – for Kohn was fond of calling on them – that he had not yet encountered the Toff.

"You will, sooner or later," she often said, "and when that happens I'll go out of black. Or I won't need it again."

And there she left it.

She admitted that Kohn was smarter than her brother had been in some ways. He knew all the tricks, and when he had a man put out of the way he did it cleanly, and yet made as sure as anyone could that it would never be traced to him. But she also knew the Toff, and was one of those people who believed he could do the impossible.

It was twenty minutes after Charlie Wray had telephoned the information to Kohn that Irma stood up, pressed out a cigarette, and moved towards the door, and the flat next to Kohn's – which flat, as a porter had told Jolly, she often deserted.

"I'll see you later," she said, "after I've patted Renway's hand again. For a millionaire, that man's the biggest louse I've met."

"He won't be a millionaire much longer," said Kohn gently.

"It'll be your fault if he is, *Mr. Brown.*"

As she spoke she reached the door, and turned the handle. For a second she stood quite rigid in the doorway, staring at something – or someone – Kohn could not see. The man saw her face pale, even beneath the rouge, and could imagine the hard glint in her eyes.

And then he heard the cool, assured, somehow mocking voice that greeted her, a voice which masked the Toff's inner excitement at hearing the name she had uttered.

"Hallo, Irma, my pet," he said. "I've been wondering when I'd see you again. What's the trouble? Come, come, can't we find a smile for an old friend?"

It was then that Kohn realized instinctively who it was, and then that the Toff advanced into the room, while Irma stepped back as if in a dream.

Chapter Five

Not Between Friends

Kohn did not speak; Irma seemed as though she could not. The Toff pushed the door to behind him, and offered cigarettes.

He smiled as he took out his case, and there was something inimitable and rakish about the crook of his brows and the twist of his lips, a something Anthea would have loved to see.

"I don't seem to be among friends," he said, "and that's a pity. Smoke? No? Another pity."

He lit a cigarette and flicked the match into the fireplace, sending a streamer of grey smoke over Irma's head as he did so. His movements were remarkably assured, and Kohn, seeing him for the first time, must have been impressed. He even sat down, hitching his trousers up to care for the crease, and he seemed quite unaware of the coldness of his greeting, or, at least, he ignored it.

Kohn kept silent deliberately; he was waiting to see how the woman would react to this unexpected encounter. The slightest sign of weakness, and his association with her would have to finish. He was surprised by the visit, but not alarmed: so far, he saw no need for being alarmed. He need not have worried about Irma, for she drew a deep breath, and flashed a smile more brilliant than Kohn had seen from her before.

"So *you're* back again, Rollison? I've been waiting for you."

"I'm always butting in when I'm not wanted," murmured the Toff. "It's a bad habit, but it has its points. Just to comfort you and your Sphinx-like friend, this is solely a social call."

"We don't have to make you welcome," said Irma.

"I hardly expect it, but I'm not really sorry. My regard for you was magnetic, sweetheart. I saw you at the Embassy last night, of course, and I couldn't resist following you. You're not surprised?"

"Not at all, but why the delay?"

"One way and the other I was busy, and had no time to see you home," said the Toff, and his smile was winning. "And I should hate to compete with so practised a veteran as Renway."

He drawled the name out, watching Kohn as he spoke. The man's face showed expression, losing its immobility for a fraction of a second; but the Toff knew malevolence when he saw it. Irma took it better than Kohn, and even smiled. She was used to the unexpected from Rollison, was getting over the first shock of meeting him face to face.

"You robbed me of my income," she said. "I've got to be fed and clothed somehow."

"Possibly," murmured the Toff, "although it's hard to see why. Renway must be a profitable golden egg for you and Kohn. It is Kohn, isn't it? Leo to friends?"

He glanced across at Kohn through narrowed mocking, eyes, and he saw the man's thin lips curl back, knowing that his self-control was being severely tested.

"I don't know who you are," snapped Kohn at last, "but I do know you've overstayed your welcome. Unless you want to talk to him, Irma?"

"A delicate hint, to be followed up by the more than possibility of my being thrown out," said Rollison.

He tossed his cigarette away. "I'll relieve you of the bother, but you know where to get me if I'm wanted. Irma does, at all events—77a Gresham Terrace, as always, my sweet, and if you come tomorrow night I may be entertaining Renway. You'd be surprised if you knew how that man likes me."

He waved a hand and moved across the room, easy, lithe, graceful. He was outside almost before Kohn realized it, and certainly before the crook had recovered from his anger.

Kohn stood up now, his face red, and his eyes blazing.

"The blasted fool! I'll get him if …"

"It's your last job on earth," said the Toff's voice languidly from the other side of the door. "Teach Leo how easily threats slide off me, Irma, it will be your good deed for the day."

The door latched gently, but Kohn walked across and turned the key in the lock, each movement slow and deliberate.

"So that was Rollison," he said, very softly. "And he's meddling in the Renway business. There's a leakage somewhere."

"Don't be silly," said Irma. "He saw me with the old fool at the Embassy, and Rollison doesn't need much encouragement to make two and two into four."

"I'll look after Rollison," snapped Kohn. "But watch Renway tonight, and stop his visit tomorrow."

"Stop him?" Irma laughed without humour, and rested a hand on Kohn's sleeve, a curiously feline gesture. "My dear Leo, either Rollison was lying to scare us, or else he's made a date with Renway. Stop Renway keeping it, and he'll want to know why."

"Rollison might make him talk."

"Don't you believe it. Renway's too anxious to keep things quiet, for more reasons than one. But get Rollison quickly, he'll be in the middle of it before long."

The passion in her voice did more to jerk Kohn out of his mood than anything else could have done. He looked at her oddly, and then shrugged.

"He's got you worried, hasn't he? Don't worry, my dear, I'll talk to Wray within the next half-hour."

"Talking won't hurt Rollison," Irma snapped.

She was by the door again, and she turned the key and opened it. She would not have been surprised had the Toff been there still, but there was no sign of him. As she stepped forward, however, her foot stubbed against an object on the floor, and she stumbled and almost fell. The thing slid along, and as she recovered herself she saw it and stared.

There seemed neither rhyme nor reason in it, and she could not reconcile it with the Toff's visit, although instinctively she knew it was connected.

"What is it?" snapped Kohn, who had heard her stumble.

"A—boot," said Irma dazedly. "And a heavy one." She picked it up, a large and hobnailed specimen, and went on: "Now I wonder just what that means?"

A telephone call to Scotland Yard about ten o'clock that night had brought to the police the information that there was something worth investigating at Noddle's Wharf, Wapping. Chief Inspector McNab, a Scotsman who was on duty many more hours than most of his colleagues, took a plain-clothes sergeant with him for the investigation, and thus found the body of Alfred Sidey.

Sidey was known to both men.

He was – or he had been – one of the few crooks who had tried their hands at a variety of things. Most stuck to one subject, McNab knew from experience; a blackmailer rarely turned his hand to burglary or counterfeiting, a conman rarely picked a pocket. Sidey had been thrice convicted in twelve years, however, and each time on a different count. McNab had also heard rumours that he was an exponent of putting on the black, and that he did not hesitate to squeal on men of his own type. Sidey, in fact, had been nobody's darling.

Now he was a corpse, and was likely to give the police as much trouble dead as alive.

McNab put the usual formalities into operation, traced the telephone call to a call-box which yielded no clue to the caller, and then decided to visit Mrs. Alfred Sidey. As he journeyed through the fog he cursed the whole affair.

The only clue was the bread-knife, one of a cheap variety probably purchased from a one-time sixpenny store, from which every print had been wiped clean.

It was police duty, of course, to advise the widow, although the Chief Inspector need not have performed it himself. But he knew

Minnie Sidey, who was a red-headed shrew, and had seen the inside of gaol as often as her husband. So far as McNab could judge, she had been running straight for a year, but she was probably in her husband's confidence, and McNab decided she was worth interrogating. The quicker the better.

Certainly, Sidey had done well.

He had lived in a flat at Lambeth, of a type that probably cost him ten pounds a week, high for that side of the river. Minnie, who had been reading a passionate love story, was annoyed at the interruption, and even more by the sight of McNab. She made this clear before McNab had entered the living-room, for which he made, leaving her standing by the open front door.

McNab was a large, chunky man, not particularly tall, who created the impression that he was an outsize in all things – except, as the Toff would say when incensed, brain power. He had a corporation of considerable proportions, and yet it did not seem overlarge. His habit of walking slowly and planting each foot down deliberately was typical of him. In all things he was deliberate, and if he never jumped to conclusions, it rarely happened that his conclusions were reached on insufficient evidence.

It occurred to him that Minnie did not want to see him, and yet she did not seem too frightened. In short, she suspected that her husband had been unlawfully busy, but had little or no knowledge of how. That was the inference, although McNab did not take it for granted.

He sat, uninvited, on the arm of the chair, and turned his sandy face towards her. His hair, and eyebrows, were also sandy, beetling over light blue eyes which could be disconcerting. He had never been known to hurry in the normal course of business.

Minnie snarled: "Get out've my house, you ruddy nark, an' ..."

"That's quite enough of that," said McNab heavily. "Come in and close the door, I want to talk to you."

"What—alone in my house with you? Whatjer take me for! I'll complain about it, I will. I'll tell them you had a go at me."

"That's all right," said McNab comfortably. "I'm not worried, my girl, and I'm not likely to be. Be sensible, now."

Minnie closed the door.

She had been in front of an electric fire, and her face was shiny and flushed with the heat. She had not painted nor powdered that evening, and her flaming red hair was tousled where her fingers had played with it. Her green eyes were glittering, and her lips, very thin and pale, were drawn tightly together. A slight woman, she seemed to have little or no figure as she planted herself in front of McNab, and she was not a sight to bewitch any man's eyes. Yet when she was dressed and ready for social occasions, Minnie Sidey was pretty, and she had an attraction for men which had frequently made her husband jealous – generally without cause.

"Well, what is it, you b—?"

"Try and ease off that language," said McNab. He spoke slowly, as if picking his words with great care. In actual fact the care was expended on the accent which was apt, on hasty occasions, to become very broad Scots.

"I'll do what I want in my own house!" retorted Minnie, and it was obvious that she was reassuring herself because she was on her own ground. "What lies are you comin' to tell me?"

McNab eyed her evenly.

"I'm not telling you lies, Mrs. Sidey. I've got some news for you that you won't like."

She stared, uncomprehending.

It was hardly likely that she would understand, and yet McNab had introduced the subject with far less callousness than might have been expected. There was another thing. Normally a policeman only visited a woman when he had company, for accusations of assault would otherwise be common and difficult to disprove. He had come alone, a strange thing for that most cautious of officers. She was suspicious of a trick, and her temper grew even more uncertain.

"Lissen, if you don't clear out ..."

"Now stop it," ordered McNab, and his own temper stirred. "It's doin' ye no good, and it's helpin' ye none. I've bad news, I told ye."

She stared, still uncomprehending, and, in fact, unable to understand his attitude at all.

"What—what kind've news? If Sidey's inside again ..."

"He isn't," said McNab, slowly, and more accentless. "He isn't going to be, Mrs. Sidey."

Her hands went to her chest.

"*What!*"

"I'm not liking the news I've got for ye," said McNab, and to do the policeman credit, he felt sorry for the woman. She knew what he was going to tell her, and was staring at him fixedly, and with an expression in her eyes that was not far removed from horror. "Sidey's been killed, Mrs. Sidey."

"*Killed!*" She breathed the word, and her hands tightened against her chest.

McNab doubted whether she had had any prior intimation, doubted whether she had suspected that such an end had been likely – which suggested that she knew little of the type of men her husband had lately been working with. He sighed inwardly, for he had hoped for information, or at least a hint that it was obtainable. No such hint was in that thin, shrewish face. Breathing heavily, she moved to a chair and sat down. Every movement was slow, and made with difficulty.

"Useless to mince words," said McNab. "He was murdered, Mrs. Sidey."

She accepted what he said, but she flinched. McNab was still trying to get the slightest hint that she had information, and now he knew that she had beaten him, for her expression remained blank, although she had contrived to pull herself together.

"You're kiddin'." Her voice was lifeless.

"Listen to me." He gave her the bare outlines of the murder, but did not tell her where the body had been found, nor how it had been discovered. She heard him out in stony silence that seemed uncanny, and when finally he finished, she said: "The lousy tykes! An' he's been on the up-and-up, Mister McNab, he's been runnin' straight. I bet he wouldn't take a job fer some blasted crook, and that's happened. That's what happens when you try to run straight. If the dicks don't frame you, yer own friends git you."

"Who are his friends?" demanded McNab craftily.

"You know, as well as I do." That was a fair answer, and McNab doubted whether she would crack under a stiffer interrogation. He was in two minds whether to take her to the Yard but decided to leave her.

There was no good reason for taking her away, and certainly not the slightest reason for treating her as a suspect. If the Press discovered that had been done, there would be trouble at the Yard. Sir Ian Warrender, the Assistant Commissioner and Head of the Criminal Investigation Department, had been told by the Home Secretary within the past ten days that due attention must be paid to all formalities – and McNab was not a man to ignore that. There was more reason than ever, in fact, why no one should have a complaint that could be splashed in the headlines.

He stood up.

"If you learn anything, let me have it quickly. Don't keep things back—it's your husband they've killed, remember that."

"I won't forget," she said, tight-lipped.

"That's right," McNab hesitated, and then said less formally, "I'm sorry, Minnie. Anything I can do?"

"No."

"Money all right?"

"If you think I'll let the bleedin' dicks pay fer his funeral, you're wrong! Get out, get out, damn you, I ..."

McNab, knowing that hysterics were near, went out quickly, but stayed by the door for some minutes. He heard first the shouting, and then the sobbing – and decided that another woman was wanted. He knocked up a neighbour, who went at once to Minnie's flat, and then walked slowly back towards Westminster Bridge and the Yard.

Had she really been upset?

Or had that scene been staged for his benefit?

He did not know, and he had to admit that he could not be sure of anything with Minnie. He sighed, for at the back of his mind there was a fear that she had put something across him. It had happened in the past, and yet there seemed no way in which he could make sure that it had not happened again.

He took all the precautions he could by having a plainclothes man detailed to duty outside the flat until further notice, while he sat back in his office and grumbled about the fog. It stopped everything, and it had made the murderer's job so much easier.

McNab had an uncomfortable feeling that things were not as they should be. It was a popular fallacy among many people that Scotland Yard had their fingers on the pulse of the underworld – which, McNab would say, was a theory that might fit if anyone knew where the underworld was. He and the other officers knew as well as Rollison that many things happened which did not reach the ears of the police – the history of the post-war years was one crime wave after another.

McNab shrugged, and decided to go down to the canteen for a cup of tea. After twenty minutes he returned, and as he opened the door his shoulders drooped a little, and he looked a tired man.

He straightened up abruptly a moment later, however, and his shaggy eyebrows moved. For there was only one voice in McNab's world quite as nonchalant as the one that addressed him unexpectedly from an armchair in front of the coal fire, in that office which normally sheltered four Chief Inspectors.

"You've kept me waiting a long time, Mac," he was assured, "and I hope you've a pick-me-up waiting."

"What are *you* doing here?" said McNab, as the Toff stood up from the chair and smiled at him.

"Only great detectives can identify men so fast," said the Toff amiably. "I always said your gifts weren't fully recognized, Mac."

"Who," demanded McNab, "let you in?"

"Whoever it was, I told him I was calling on you by appointment, so don't start reducing him to the ranks."

McNab knew Rollison well – too well at times – and he needed no telling that a visit so late on a foggy night was important. Most of the things which the Toff discussed with McNab were important, or they developed in a big way. If the Inspector did not approve of the Toff's methods, he admitted their efficacy, and at times they were on friendly terms.

"Well," he demanded, as they both sat down, Rollison looking as if he owned the place, "what do you want?"

"That's all the reward I get," said the Toff, "for reporting a murder an hour after it was committed. Are all Scotsmen as mean-minded as you, Mac?"

McNab did not let him finish, but demanded a full story. The Toff thereon explained a little, but McNab guessed he was holding a great deal back.

According to the Toff's statement, he had been prowling about the wharves when he had heard a scuffle and a cry. He had investigated and seen the dead man and chased after the murderer.

"I lost him in the fog, Mac, it's just as simple as that. I hate to admit it, but there it is."

"I doubt you've told me everything," said McNab dubiously, "but I know you won't until you're ready."

The Toff's expression changed to one of bland innocence, and with that McNab had to be satisfied; but he still doubted whether the Toff had confided more than a bare outline, and he started his report in a glum frame of mind. It seemed that both Minnie Sidey and the Hon. Richard Rollison were holding out on him – which was not far from the truth.

Chapter Six

Of Many Things

There were many things on the Toff's mind as he made his way back to Gresham Terrace, and one of them was the possibility that Irma and Kohn would begin to act against him tonight. Once they started he knew that they would be serious about it, and since he was convinced that Kohn, as Mr. Brown, was connected with Sidey's murder – via Benson and perhaps via Irma – there was every reason to believe that his death would be preferred to his company.

He had few illusions about Kohn – although more about that impressive-looking man with the high forehead than about Irma, however, for he had never met Kohn, until that night. He judged him to be as ruthless as Irma, and perhaps more clever. Certainly Irma lacked the "something" to make a Big Shot, although she was an admirable lieutenant.

Rollison looked up and down Gresham Terrace, which was off Brook Street, before he entered the house where his flat was on the first floor. He saw no lurking figures, and only two pedestrians, and it seemed that he was not yet being watched; he would be before the night was out, or he had over-estimated Kohn's prowess.

He rang the bell of his flat, and Jolly opened the door. There were few occasions when the Toff went into his flat with his key while an affair was in progress: he knew the possibility of an unexpected guest waiting to welcome him. The simple things, the old-tried methods, were the ones more likely to succeed against him; he knew that well enough and took the necessary precautions.

Jolly stepped towards the cocktail cabinet.

"I wonder why," said the Toff, not a little testily, "you always make a beeline for that, Jolly? Do I strike you as a toper, a two-bottle man, or …?"

"You look tired, sir."

"I don't believe it," said the Toff.

Thereon he stepped into the bathroom and examined himself in the mirror at close quarters. He disliked admitting it, or affected to, but he did look tired. There were lines at his eyes which should not be there, and the eyes themselves looked heavy. He shrugged his shoulders, washed, and went back into the living-room, where Jolly had poured out whisky and soda. The Toff drank, without comment.

"Well, Jolly, what have you been doing?"

"Nothing of much value, sir"

"Hmm. Kohn?"

"There is little information about him, sir. He is English, of a German father and an Austrian mother."

"Very English indeed," said the Toff, cocking an eyebrow.

"His father was naturalized in nineteen hundred and three," said Jolly, with a slightly disapproving note in his voice, "and the child, of course, took on his father's nationality. Kohn was educated at Charterhouse …"

"Was he, by Jove!"

"And went to America, where he finished off his education at Yale. He returned to this country, an orphan, in nineteen twenty-one, and has since travelled a great deal. He is reputedly rich, although his father's source of income is not disclosed, and it is not known whether much money was left to Leopold Kohn, sir. Kohn has been in England for some six months, and Miss Cardew for three. Miss Cardew, I understand, was not living at the Arch Mansions flat until ten weeks ago."

"Hmm," said the Toff. "So that's all you know about our Leo?"

"I'm afraid so, sir," said Jolly, and he sounded genuinely apologetic. There was reason, for although the Toff had given him instructions to find all that it was possible to find about Irma's new mentor, the idea – as Jolly knew well – had been to try to trace his recent activities. About that there was nothing to report.

"I see," said the Toff. "Not bad, on the whole. How did you manage to get hold of his history?"

"I learned from the porter at the flats that he employed an old servant when he first went to the Mansions, but afterwards dismissed the servant without a pension. The servant was old, sir, somewhere near seventy. I paid him five pounds for this information."

"It was worth it. Would ten bring any more?"

"No, sir, not in my opinion. The servant, a naturalized German named Schmidt, does not appear to have a high opinion of his late employer, whom he complains gambles excessively, and is often without money. But he continues to live well."

"Ye-es. Keep an eye, or let someone else keep an eye, on friend Schmidt. Now what about Renway?"

"Nothing very startling, sir. You know most of what there is to know. He has recently retired from business …"

"What?"

"He has retired from business, and …"

"Are you sure?"

Jolly looked hurt.

"Of course, sir. May I ask why you consider the question necessary?"

"Yes, you may. Sir Matthew Waterer claimed that it was past time that Renway retired, and suggested that he was no longer fit for business, Jolly. How long have these retirements been effective?"

"He was on the boards of several companies, sir, and relinquished the last in the spring of this year. The Bi-National Electric Corporation, I am told."

"Hmm—a sound enough concern," said the Toff, who knew something about companies, particularly those which were in any way unsound. "Right, Jolly, it will all help. You may now listen to me."

Jolly listened, proving a better listener than the Toff, for he made no interruptions. When the Toff had given him a resume of his adventures, Jolly remained silent for some seconds, and then pulled tentatively at his underlip.

"Why did you see McNab, sir?"

"Why not?" asked the Toff, and then more generously: "It was as well, Jolly. I want to know all I can about this business, and we're by no means sure of getting to the Sidey angle now that Sidey is dead. McNab can help us more about him than we can help ourselves, and we'll know just what he has been doing of late. If the police know, of course, which is by no means a certainty. However, we can but live in hope. The main issues, then, Jolly, are: "First—Irma and Kohn are working on Renway.

"Second—Renway is lousy with money, without-business interests, with one nephew—we haven't met him yet—and an eye for beauty as represented by Irma. Also a collection of Old Masters is in his possession.

"Three—Charlie Wray is concerned in the business, and his man, Benson, killed Sidey …"

"Is that a fact, sir?"

"You may accept it as one, but I haven't enough evidence to take to McNab, and if I had I doubt whether I would. I want to save that for the time being, Jolly, it might be useful if we ever want to talk to Benson. Don't interrupt, and where was I? Oh, yes:

"Four—Wray does not approve of my sudden interest, and doubtless will soon suspect something about the boot."

"Dare I ask, sir, what boot?"

"My dear Jolly," said the Toff with some show of indignation, "the boot is the key to the whole business, the one thing that lifts it out of the rut. Sidey was killed by Benson, when Benson had nothing on his feet but socks. If he wears socks. I wonder how many other murders have been committed with stockinged feet? Or by a man wearing no shoes or boots? Try to visualize the psychological effect of that boot which I gave to Irma—she stumbled over it—and the fact that there is another boot missing. Imagine what happens to Benson and Charlie Wray when they know all about the boot I sent back, and nothing about the boot I still hold. They'll know that someone was close enough at hand to see and hear that murder, it will have them so jittery that they'll always be looking over their shoulder. Have I made the significance of the boot clear?"

"Perfectly, sir, thank you."

"Right. Then we're all set for sparks. Irma and Kohn are in the middle of something, they would not kill at the end of a show—not that way, anyhow. We've got them worried, which means they'll get active. We're to be prepared for all emergencies, Jolly, until Kohn and Irma are no longer worrying us."

"Yes, sir."

"And now," said the Toff, "there is the matter of Renway. I have telephoned him, and he's coming to see me. I told Irma about that, and she wasn't pleased."

"Dare I ask why you told her, sir?"

"You dare. It's all part of the Rollison service," said the Toff, sipping at his whisky again, and lighting a cigarette. "It will make them move hurriedly, and when in a hurry things are apt to be done carelessly. I'm expecting an attack or assault at any moment, remember that."

"Yes, sir. You were talking of Mr. Renway."

"Was I? Oh, yes. I want an Italian panel that I think is by de Rossi. Renway is coming to see it, and to advise me. So get out quickly, and buy the cheapest imitation of a de Rossi that you can find. An old one, preferably, you'll get one in the Strand, if nowhere else. All understood?"

"Yes, sir," said Jolly. "I'll go at once."

Rollison sat back for some minutes, and then stood up and examined himself in the bathroom mirror again. He grimaced, for he did not like to think that he was tired at the beginning of an affair. There were, of course, good reasons. Prior to the arrival of Anthea there had been several quick *affaires*, and the Toff had spent ten days on the social whirl. They included very late nights, and he could do with some sleep.

Renway, however, was due at seven.

The Toff bathed, leisurely, still pondering the murder and the motive behind it, and was rubbing himself down when the telephone rang. He draped a towel about him and went into the living room, to hear a pleasing feminine voice which he recognized immediately.

"Mr. Rollison, please."

"And you really don't know me?" mourned the Toff.

"Oh—Rolly!" Anthea's voice sounded relieved, and a moment later her words confirmed it. "Are you all right?"

"Of course I'm all right."

"I—I had an awful fear that something might have gone wrong."

"Don't get that kind of anxiety-complex," said the Toff laughingly, although he did not feel amused. He hoped that Anthea was not going to become too attached, and he groaned when she went on: "I'm not sure about that. Rolly, Jamie's been delayed."

"Oh," said Rollison. "Too bad."

"And I'm alone, cooped up in the house because of my beastly ankle."

"I'm awfully sorry," said the Toff, who seemed off form conversationally.

"Ye-es," said Anthea, and she laughed a little. "You're blessing me, aren't you, Rolly? Wishing I wouldn't pester you, and hoping I won't fall for your grey eyes! There's no need for worry there, either; Jamie's just right for me, but …" she paused for a moment, and when she went on sounded a little forlorn: "If you have a little while to spare tonight, or tomorrow, I'd love to hear what's happening."

You would, would you?" said Rollison, and he laughed, for there was something very appealing about Anthea. "I'll see what I can do for you, my infant, but don't expect too much. And if I come, remember that I'm already in bad with your mother."

"You're not. I told her about the visiting card, and she …"

"I can see my sympathy is wasted on you," Rollison said. "Nevertheless, I'll slip round if I can."

"I'd love you to, Rolly! Goodbye."

Rollison replaced the receiver, arched his eyebrows, shrugged, and then turned away from the telephone. He was feeling chilly, and he stepped towards the bathroom, still a little uncertain in his mind about Anthea. She was an amazingly fresh youngster – fresh in the vivid sense – and yet although she laughed at the idea, it remained a possibility that she was thinking about him too seriously.

It was the last kind of complication that Rollison wanted.

He finished drying himself, dressed quickly in a dinner-jacket, and then stepped from his bedroom to the living-room. Jolly was not yet back, but it did not occur to the Toff that his man would fail to get the picture. Renway, however, was due at seven, and it was now a quarter to.

The telephone rang again, abruptly.

Rollison lifted the receiver, thinking of Anthea – and then he forgot her completely, although it was a woman's voice, and one he would have recognized anywhere, at any time.

"Rollison …"

"Ye-es," said the Toff very gently. "A moment, while I get a chair. I shall love a chat with you."

"You won't need a chair," said Irma Cardew abruptly. "You'll need wood made up into a box unless you get out of London quickly."

"My dear Irma!" Rollison sounded genuinely startled, and in truth he was. "You're not trying that very old one, are you?"

"I'm telling you the truth," said Irma, icily.

The Toff hesitated for a moment, completely at sea. He did not believe that Irma would telephone him to tell him that he was being advised to leave London. It was the kind of puerile threat which some men – and women – made when they first met him, but Irma would not make that mistake. There was an ulterior purpose, and he could not see what it was.

"You heard me," she went on, still sharply. "I'm not fooling, Rollison."

"No-o. What was it you really wanted to say?"

"I've said it," said Irma, and then she drew a deep breath – one audible enough for Rollison to hear. "Rollison, I'm going to marry Renway."

"Yes?"

"Don't talk like that! I need the money, and …"

"If I could think it were all," said Rollison with a mocking note in his voice, "I might almost wish you God-speed. But I know differently, and …"

It was then that the door of the room, leading to the hall, opened. It opened stealthily, and the Toff would have heard nothing since he was speaking and listening, but he was sitting facing the door. And suddenly he knew the real purpose of this call, and even then he silently applauded Irma, for it was very clever.

"Rollison, please don't interfere!" Her voice sounded desperate, and another man than Rollison might have believed in the sincerity of her appeal. Rollison said, more loudly than before and watching the door all the time: "My dear, sweet girl, I hate interfering and you know it. But I need a lot more evidence than I've got that you're going to be a virtuous woman, and settle down to marrying Renway. I wonder if he knows that you've been acquitted—by error—of a murder charge, and ..."

He went on talking.

Most of what he said was nonsense, the kind of nonsense he was apt to talk at some length. But he was watching the door closely all the time, and he saw the hand that appeared round it. A hand holding a gun.

He paused for a moment, and as silence descended the gun disappeared. The door was open only just wide enough for the gun and hand to get through.

Irma said something, and Rollison hardly knew what it was.

He slid his own right hand to his coat pocket after transferring the telephone to the left, and drew out an automatic. He talked back, and as he started speaking the gun showed again. He felt on tenterhooks as he levelled his own gun towards the hand at the door. "And then," he said to Irma, "I might believe you. But not now, certainly not now."

The brim of a hat showed at the door, which was opening slowly, stealthily.

"Rollison, listen to me, I want ..."

And then the man at the door came through, his finger on the trigger of his automatic, while Rollison squeezed his own trigger at the same time. Two flashes of flame, two silenced shots – and the telephone crashed from Rollison's hand.

Chapter Seven

Renway is Sorrowful

In the Toff's life things happened swiftly or not at all; or at least it seemed that way. The moments of preparation, the seconds which had seemed like hours while the man at the door had waited for the best moment to shoot were forgotten.

There was the gunman reeling back behind the door, while his gun hit the carpet. There was the Toff, his left wrist strained by the way the telephone had been shattered in his grasp. It was in pieces, now, on the floor. And the shock at his wrist, stabbing through him and momentarily sending him off his balance, stopped him from moving as fast as he wanted.

The door banged as he started for it.

He had struck the gunman's automatic and not his wrist; he knew that, for he had seen no sign of blood. Now he hesitated for a split second, uncertain whether there were more men outside. He heard a man hurrying downwards, and took a chance and opened the door quickly.

No one was in sight, but a trilby hat was lying by the wall.

The Toff went through – and then the Toff had one of those falls which he frequently claimed were good for him. He struck something with his shin without knowing what it was, and went sprawling forward. He put his shoulder down to break the impact, and the fall did not even wind him. But it lost him precious seconds, and when he stood up and hurried to the head of the stairs he knew that it was too late for him to catch the gunman.

He went down, however, and looked along Gresham Terrace.

The red rear light of a car was disappearing into Brook Street and it seemed reasonable to assume that it carried his man. Certainly it was reasonable to believe that he, Rollison, could not catch up, no matter how he tried, and in a chastened frame of mind he went back to his flat.

The thing that had tripped him was a piece of cord, tied across the doorway. Obviously, the gunman had prepared for pursuit, and dealt with the likelihood accordingly. About that attempt to kill him there was a thoroughness which the Toff, who could look at many things in a detached frame of mind, was compelled – wholly without approval – to admire.

He straightened his clothes, combed his hair, and then went thoughtfully to the telephone in his bedroom. It was a separate line, and not an extension, and he got through to the operator without trouble. He reported a damaged instrument, and then asked for a Mayfair number – the number of Irma's flat. There was some delay before she answered.

"My sweet," said the Toff in his most honeyed voice, "I am going to wring your neck for that."

He heard Irma gasp.

That in itself was an achievement, and did something to restore his self-respect, for he knew that it was her first intimation that the attack had failed. He went on: "I let your little man get away, Irma, as I can put him in jail when I want to. I saw that murder, you know—the Sidey murder. But I haven't quite connected him up with you and Kohn, and I don't propose to risk another acquittal. Am I understood?"

"I don't know what you're talking about," Irma said harshly.

"Don't you, my darling? Think hard, and it might pierce the little grey cells. My love to Leo, and tell Benson I think he's a punk gunman."

"I don't know ..."

"What I'm talking about, of course. You said so before," went on the Toff, "and doubtless you'll say it when you're in a dock on a murder charge which you can't wriggle out of. It's after the trial that I'm going to squeeze your lovely neck, metaphorically. The silken hemp will tighten very quickly, Irma, which is a pity in some ways, I think; there ought to be a method of prolonging the deed for ladies like you, and gentlemen like Leo. Oh, and before I go—has Benson found his other boot yet?"

Irma used words which were not nice from a lady, and the Toff reproved her before he rang down abruptly, smoothed his hair, and glanced at his watch.

It wanted two minutes to seven.

Rollison frowned, for Jolly had not yet returned and he suspected that Renway was one of those impossible men who are always punctual. It was unlike Jolly to be late, and the Toff wondered whether it was possible that an accident, in the way of an attack, had befallen him. There was nothing that could be done at that moment to investigate, and the Toff picked up the pieces of the broken telephone, frowned, and then cut the wire close to the wall. It would have been difficult to explain the damaged instrument to Renway; he would not have been able to miss seeing it when he arrived.

It was now seven o'clock precisely.

The front-door bell rang, and Rollison's estimate of Renway's punctuality proved right. Renway came in, a man of medium height, well wrapped in a heavy coat, wearing a trilby pulled down over his forehead, mufflered, and yet obviously cold. The room was warm, and the Toff shepherded his guest to a chair near the fire and busied himself at the cocktail cabinet. He asked questions …

"Sherry, please, Rollison. Very dry. Can you manage that, I wonder? So many of you younger people seem to think that sherry is a drink of the past, but believe me …"

"Amontillado," said the Toff amiably.

"Oh, excellent, excellent."

The Toff, with one eye on the door, felt considerable relief, for Renway was not going to demand to see the picture immediately.

Would Jolly come in time? And if he failed, would Renway be easily put off with apologies?

It was not, thought the Toff, a good moment.

He studied Renway as the latter sat back, warming his feet in front of the wide electric fire. A stouter man than he had first appeared to Rollison, there was no doubting the lines of worry at his eyes and mouth. He seemed older than he was, for the Toff had discovered that he was not yet sixty, while he would have passed for a man of seventy anywhere. His hair was more white than grey, his eyes were watery and red-rimmed, and he looked as if he suffered from insomnia. His skin was white and puffy, and he had every appearance of a sick man. A faint blueness at his nose suggested to the Toff that Renway might suffer from a weak heart; the lobes of his ears suggested the same thing.

His voice was mellow and pleasant, however, and untroubled.

He was dressed in a dinner-jacket of old-fashioned cut, and made no attempt to ape youth – which was a little surprising in a man who was setting his cap at so youthful a beauty as Irma. Everything about Paul Renway, in fact – even before he started talking – suggested that he was a self-made man who cared nothing for appearances.

"Take me for what I am," he seemed to say, "that's all I want."

The Toff, seeing this, was not displeased, but he was getting more concerned about the missing de Rossi. Could one invite an expert to pass judgement on a picture which was not there?

"Ve-ry, ve-ry good," said Renway, holding his glass up and regarding the amber liquid with an appreciative eye. "I'm glad to know that all modern taste is not debased, Rollison. These fiendish cocktails—paugh!"

"They show," said the Toff, leaping at the opportunity, "the effects of a speed-crazy world. Neurosis rules the land, the youngsters don't know whether they're coming or going, excitement—spirits— fun and games all the time. It's deplorable."

"An admirable sentiment, Rollison, admirable! You know, when you telephoned me about that picture …"

The Toff held his breath, but retained a poker face.

"About that picture," repeated Renway, as if with malice, "I was most interested, Rollison. I've heard many rumours about you, you know. Queer stories."

"Ah," thought the Toff, "I'm saved." Aloud: "Have you?"

"Oh, yes. Quite a reputation in your way, I'm told. A strange habit, investigating crime. It is a habit, of course? Of course," added Paul Renway, turning the question into a statement, "but it can be assumed that you find considerable interest in it. Types, I assume. Peculiar types of men about, of course. I've always known that. Evolution, eh?" He pronounced the word as if it was his own coining, quite obviously finding it an absorbing topic.

The minutes passed, and the Amontillado sank lower in the bottle. Three cigarettes disappeared, and no Jolly had arrived; there was no picture.

"Yes," said Renway reflectively, "I'm not usually eager to make new acquaintances, Rollison; at my time of life one knows one's friends. Frankly, I would have refused to come to see any man but yourself about that de Rossi. However, I felt that a chat would be most instructive. Most instructive. What time is it?"

"Just on a quarter to eight," said the Toff, and prepared himself for the worst.

"A quarter to—God bless my soul! I'm due at the Embassy at eight o'clock, Rollison. That picture, quickly, please. I'll be putting my coat on."

Rollison stood up, groaning inwardly, assisted Renway with his coat, spent some seconds looking for his hat and finally felt that some kind of act must be staged.

"It won't take a moment, Renway, and you're only five minutes from the Embassy on foot. My man will get it."

He went to the fireplace and pressed the bell.

He knew that Jolly would not come; he wondered how he would extricate himself from this impossible situation, for Renny was already looking impatiently at his watch. Rollison was inventing what seemed to him the most likely story, that his man was under notice and thoroughly unreliable, when the door opened and Jolly entered.

The Toff stared.

"You rang, sir?" said Jolly deferentially.

"Er—yes, Jolly. That …"

"The picture, sir?" said Jolly. "I will get it at once, sir. A moment, sir."

He retired to the kitchen quarters, while Renway looked again at his watch, and the Toff brushed his hand over his forehead and silently blessed and yet cursed Jolly. But what mattered was that the picture arrived.

Renway took one glance at it.

"My dear Rollison! To think *that* a de Rossi. It's not even a good imitation. I'm sorry, my dear fellow, extremely sorry. Now … look here, come round and see me tomorrow, I'll show you some genuine pieces. Wonderful pieces," added Renway reverently. "Do come."

"I'll be delighted."

"Excellent, excellent."

Renway nodded, and Jolly opened the door – that from which the shooting had taken place, not the one through which Renway had entered – and then he suddenly darted through into the hallway. Renway stared in astonishment, while the Toff gulped – and something, somewhere, snapped with a *twang*!

"Excuse me, sir," said Jolly, returning, poker-faced.

Rollison showed Renway downstairs, and to his car.

As the Daimler drove off he drew a deep breath, and returned to his flat to find Jolly stooping down and picking up the cord, which was broken in the middle.

"Jolly," said the Toff slowly, "there is something the matter with me. I forgot that possibility."

"I saw it just in time, sir," said Jolly. "If you will excuse me, I will put a little iodine on the graze which the breaking of it caused." He bowed and retired, and returned to find the Toff contemplating the pieces of the broken telephone.

"Was everything satisfactory, sir?"

"Nearly," said the Toff. "I've seen Renway, and struck up an acquaintance that will be useful in the future. He's tired, and I think he's worried, but he's very self-satisfied. Jolly, why didn't you let me know you were back?"

"I returned only a few minutes before you rang, sir. There was considerable difficulty in obtaining the picture."

Rollison smiled crookedly.

"Trust you to have an answer, eh? Well, it worked. And, Jolly, Irma sent a nasty gunman, named Benson, I fancy, to shoot me. Instead, he gave the works to the telephone."

"The anticipated violence, sir, is beginning."

"Ye-es," said the Toff. "Jolly, I'm going to Lady Anthea Munro's flat for an hour. Slip along to the Embassy and make sure that Irma and Renway are there together."

"Very good, sir. There—er—there is one other thing."

"Hmm-hmm?"

"The dealer who sold me the picture, sir, told me that Mr. Renway is a frequent visitor. I introduced the subject discreetly, of course. There was a point of interest which I felt should be passed on. Mr. Renway and his nephew have been quarrelling a great deal of late."

"Have they?" said the Toff, very thoughtfully. "Nephew and heir, isn't it?"

"Presumably, sir."

"And they're bad friends. Over what?"

"The nephew's choice of a lady friend does not please Mr. Renway, sir."

The Toff snorted – literally – and when he recovered himself he congratulated Jolly, after that worthy had assured him there was no more information that might be usefully obtained from the art dealer. But to Rollison the piece of gossip was significant indeed. Irma might have excellent reasons for wanting an estrangement between Renway and his nephew.

Could the unknown girl and cause of the trouble be working with Irma?

Chapter Eight

Family Discord Brewing

Anthea's ankle was behaving badly, and a doctor had ordered her to take two days in bed. It was the only way, as he knew, of making sure that Anthea rested completely. Consequently when the Toff called, he was shown up to Anthea's bedroom, a large, delightfully furnished apartment which seemed to express the spirit of her. She was sitting at ease, propped up with pillows, and reading a heavy-looking novel. She had given instructions that Rollison was to be sent up without being announced, and she had not expected him at that moment.

"Rolly!" The book went to the floor, as Anthea extended both hands. He took them, leaned forward, and kissed her brow with exaggerated tenderness, then stood back to regard her.

"My child, you look ill."

"Idiot," said Anthea. "I've never been better. So you're still alive?"

"Read the *Stop Press* for the first intimation of my demise," said Rollison. "It's wearying, my sweet, to feel that you're waiting expectantly for news that I've passed on."

"Don't fool, please," said Anthea. "Rolly, *can* you really be serious?"

"Occasionally, yes."

"Well, try to be now, and don't laugh at me. I can't help feeling that if you hadn't taken me out yesterday you wouldn't be in the middle of – of whatever you are in now. You see?"

Rollison was silent for a moment, and his eyes were no longer faintly mocking.

"Yes, my dear, I see. I didn't realise that was how you were looking at the situation. You needn't, any longer. This started when I saw the woman in black at the Embassy."

"Yes, I know, but you wouldn't have been at the Embassy if I hadn't been with you."

The smile came back to Rollison's eyes.

"Don't be too sure of that. I have been there before, and not alone. And in any case, Irma and I would have met; it was quite inevitable."

"I—see. Well, anyhow—is there anything I can do to help?"

"Would it cheer you up?"

"Good heavens, yes!"

"It's not in the front line," said the Toff, and it may depend on that ankle of yours. But I'm interested in a young man named Wrightson. James Wrightson, I think, so you ought to be on your home ground. "I can't tell you any more about him than that he's not popular with his family because of a lady to whom he has become attached," went on the Toff, with his habit of talking almost pedantically and yet making what he said sound amusing. "All I want to know is whether he's serious about the lady, and whether she has any kind of reputation, good or bad."

"That should be easy," said Anthea. "I know one or two Wrightsons, but I'm not sure of their Christian names. I'll phone round to some friends for inquiries, Rolly."

"Good girl. But before you do I want your word, my sweet, that you do nothing beyond what I've asked you, and do not mention my name."

"I won't."

"Promise?"

"Cross my heart," said Anthea.

"Good girl!" repeated the Toff, and meant it.

He left Anthea after an hour, knowing that she was considerably cheered. He was cheered himself, for he had been afraid that her interest in him had been mainly personal. It was a relief to know that this was not so. He could, however, easily understand that a girl of Anthea's type would blame herself for precipitating the affair on which he was engaged.

A nice person, Anthea.

He hoped her Jamie was worthy of her, hoped too that she would make some discoveries about James Wrightson – who, of course, was Paul Renway's nephew. He considered that one way and the other, he was making all the progress that he could expect.

Leopold Kohn and Irma, for instance, were not likely to be feeling on top of the world.

He smiled sombrely, and walked along Park Lane to Arch Mansions. He went up the stairs, stopped outside Kohn's door, drew out his wallet and selected one of the little cards which he had shown to Anthea. He slipped it under the door, hesitated for a moment, and then decided that he would let Kohn find it later. That done, he went back to Gresham Terrace and considered the position – a thing he was doing more often than his reputation made likely.

In the life of Leopold Kohn so many things had seemed simple.

The outline of his upbringing and education was accurate – Jolly's information, through the old servant, had been well founded. But Charterhouse and Yale had contributed nothing towards making Kohn a gentleman nice to know.

There was in him a streak of ruthlessness too often found in the Prussian – for his father HAD been a Prussian – which enabled him to consider killing as a minor incident, provided it was the killing of someone else, preferably by someone else. Only twice had Kohn's own hands been soiled by murder, but at least a dozen murders were directly attributable to him.

He had operated as a confidence trickster on a scale rarely conceived before in America, France, Monaco, India and South Africa. He used men of the Benson kind frequently, and he had a valuable connection among such criminals in many capitals. It was his habit, if any man appeared to become dangerous by demanding more than Kohn cared to pay him, to arrange his murder; he had done just that with Sidey, and would have no hesitation in doing the same thing with Benson or Charlie Wray if the need arose.

Operating in London for the first time, he had discovered in Renway an excellent victim, in Irma a perfect bait for Renway, and until that night when Irma had been seen at the Embassy, the affair had appeared to be progressing well. Since then, and since the Toff's visits, too many things had misfired.

There was the disturbing appearance of the boot, for instance, a story from Wray about Benson's nervousness, and the fact that the Toff had been seen in the East End.

The acquaintance that Rollison was striking up with Renway, too, was far from reassuring.

The decision to get Rollison out of the way quickly, Irma's idea of keeping Rollison on the phone while he was shot from the door had seemed one that could not fail, but it *had* failed – and Kohn was beginning to feel the effect of the Toff, beginning to understand why Irma hated him so bitterly, to know something of the thing which the Toff called psychological terrorism.

Kohn was considering the situation, which meant that he was considering the Toff. Irma was at the Embassy again with Renway, for the millionaire had to be kept sweet. Kohn would have preferred to talk with Irma, and even contemplated going to the Embassy on some excuse that would hold water.

And then he saw the card beneath the door.

It was lying with the little drawing upwards, and he stooped down slowly, stared at it – and the colour drained from his face. Rollison would have been the most satisfied man in the world had he seen the effect of that card on Leopold Kohn.

"The ..." said Kohn, and there was murderous viciousness in his voice as he turned back to his desk and sat down heavily. He took a decanter of whisky, poured himself out a drink, and took it neat. His hand was still a little unsteady, and he cursed himself for it – but he was not the first man and would not be the last to feel the effect of the Toff when the Toff was a long way away from him.

Renway and Irma had returned from the Embassy before midnight, Jolly reported, and Irma had gone straight to her flat.

"Nothing to do now, then, but sleep," said Rollison.

He slept until nine, and felt the better for it. The day turned out to be one of those when everything seemed at a standstill. He did not propose to go out and look for trouble: better to let Kohn and Irma stew for a while, for he believed the utlimate brew would be one disastrous for them both.

Anthea telephoned at four o'clock.

She had a little news, for she had located a James Wrightson, who was the nephew of that stuffy old millionaire, named Renway. Was that the man? The Toff said it was, and Anthea rang off so quickly that the Toff knew she was eager to get her teeth into the job.

In truth, he had wanted to keep her mind occupied, and through that get information which he or Jolly could obtain with little effort. There was, of course, the feminine angle of the Wrightson love-affair, which might prove useful and which Anthea would diagnose better than they could.

At five, Rollison presented himself at Renway's St. John's Wood house.

Renway was affability itself, made many sly digs at the gullibility of men who knew nothing about Art, and showed Rollison some of his collection.

Rollison's ignorance was not as great as Renway imagined, and Rollison was impressed. He recognised that in the present state of the market, the value of the pictures was likely to be enormous. He could not fail to see the reason for Irma's and Kohn's interest. He made the necessary admiring comments, and was then led to a small library.

It was a pleasantly furnished room, panelled in light oak. A glance about the shelves told Rollison that although Renway might be an expert on the Renaissance period as far as pictures were concerned, his literary pretensions were not high. There were, of course, the classics, leather-bound, and of the type of edition rarely read. One section of the library was filled with modern novels, mostly on the light side; there were plenty of thrillers and even light romances. It was ordinary, average taste, and it reflected no more credit on Renway than his choice of Irma as a bride.

Could that be serious? wondered the Toff.

He had let Renway get away with it fairly easily so far, but as the other brought out sherry, and was obviously prepared to be expansive, Rollison put a few gentle, leading questions. He found Renway almost maudlin on the subject of women, although he did not make any direct personal comments.

"Young and old, all get it sooner or later," said Rollison. "I suppose the older a man is the better his judgment as far as women are concerned. Particularly the woman he's thinking of marrying."

Renway frowned.

"Yes, Rollison, you're right. My nephew, now, the young fool. He's getting himself tied up with a woman who won't be the slightest use to him in the future. Oh, she's pretty enough now, but she's got no intelligence. It can't be denied that intelligence is far more important than physical attraction." Renway uttered the statement with the air of one who had thought of it before any of his fellow men, and went on worriedly: "It will have to stop. He's spending too much money, far too much of my money. He doesn't seem to appreciate the importance of conserving money, and ...", Renway broke off for a moment, and the Toff was almost afraid that the stream of confidences would dry up. But Renway went on slowly, and without prompting.

"Money doesn't make money, Rollison, in spite of fools who like to think that adage worth following. Money means work, care, consideration, judging the right moment to sell, the right to buy. I resigned from several companies at a time when I considered they were on the down grade, and that their Board was not following a money-making policy. In each case I was proved right."

Rollison raised his eyebrows, and said with the air of a man inviting a confidence which he would regard as a favour: "Is that so, Renway? Can I take it as a hint?"

Renway looked at him squarely.

"What company are you interested in?"

"I'm holding a big parcel of Bi-National Electric."

"Oh ..." Renway hesitated, and then rested a scrawny hand on Rollison's arm. "Don't worry about Bi-Nationals, they're as safe as any industrials in the country. I retired from there for private reasons. But don't run away with the idea that I'm finished with business, Rollison. I've heard it said that I'm retiring because I'm old. But the older the fox the craftier. I've something up my sleeve that people like Waterer won't forget in a hurry. I've left business, but I'm coming back with a bang, and …"

He broke off, abruptly, and to Rollison it seemed that he was almost frightened. He muttered something under his breath which was inaudible, and then added clearly: "All this is in the strictest confidence, Rollison. I'm sure I can rely on you."

"You can, completely," said the Toff, and his manner was sufficiently reassuring to make Renway relax.

"Excellent, excellent! And I'll forget the fact that you bought a cheap imitation of a de Rossi for the real thing, eh?" He laughed, and patted Rollison on the back, then suggested that they should go into his study where – he said – he kept the only sherry worth drinking in the house. "Amontillado, of course, on a par with yours, Rollison."

The Toff was interested in Amontillado just then only in so far as it might help to loosen Renway's tongue, and he doubted whether it would. On the whole, however, he could not complain. He knew more about the domestic discord which was blowing up and a little about a new business venture which Renway wanted to keep secret.

Which of those two things was of importance to Irma? Or was it those pictures?

Renway opened the door of his study, and then stopped abruptly on the threshold. He hesitated, as if uncertain whether to go in, then stepped through quickly. Rollison understood why when he saw the young man who was sitting at a desk, writing.

This, then, was the nephew.

Rollison saw the frown on young Wrightson's face as he stood up quickly. Also he covered what he had been writing, and to the Toff it seemed likely that it was a letter to his lady.

"Hallo, Uncle."

"Hm. James, meet Mr. Richard Rollison. Rollison, my nephew, James Wrightson."

Wrightson nodded, stiffly, and started for the door.

"Don't let me drive you away, please," said the Toff quickly. "I'm not staying long."

Wrightson hesitated, and glanced towards his uncle. To the Toff it seemed as if he was trying to gauge which the older man would prefer – for him to stay, or to go. Renway did nothing to help him, and Wrightson turned back into the room, taking cigarettes from his pocket and proffering them.

Renway refused, abruptly.

The Toff took one, and struck a match. Wrightson lit his cigarette, and as he did so the Toff looked closely at his face.

"Thanks," said Wrightson stiffly, and drew back. "Has Uncle been showing you the collection?"

"Yes." Rollison talked of it enthusiastically, and decided that in spite of a marked lack of response he liked the look of Wrightson. He was a little shorter than the Toff, but broader across the shoulders; and he had a rugged face that could be called attractive, but certainly not handsome. His hair was fair and crisp, and his lips well-shaped and generous. His whole expression at the moment was one of resentful sullenness.

Yet he did not look the type of man to be habitually bad-tempered.

That there was an estrangement between the uncle and the nephew would have been obvious even had the Toff not possessed prior information. Both men created the impression that they were finding it an effort to be polite to each other. The Toff chatted for a few minutes, the better to gauge the atmosphere of the house, then made his excuses.

When he left he was all smiles and thanks, but his smile disappeared as he climbed into his Frazer-Nash.

"There's a flare-up coming in that quarter," he mused. "I wonder if Irma *has* been fanning the flames?"

He meditated on the three obvious possibilities as he drove to his flat. One, that Irma was actually contemplating marriage with Renway for the sake of his money. Two, that the new business surprise that Renway had talked about was being 'nursed' by Irma and Kohn. That would be one explanation of Renway's need for secrecy. Three, that there was a plan afoot to steal the art treasures.

For the first, there was some evidence. Possibly Irma had helped to widen the older man's breach with his nephew over the association with a girl, hoping to get James Wrightson disinherited. On the other hand, neither this nor the possible art theft was the kind of crime Irma was likely to specialise in. The business angle was the one to concentrate on, as far as Rollison could judge. But while concentrating he would keep an open mind.

Meanwhile, he doubted whether trouble between Renway and Wrightson would come to a head quickly.

The Toff might have revised that opinion – or, at least, suspended it – had he been at the millionaire's house twenty minutes after he had driven off. Renway returned to the study, and his first words were anything but conciliatory.

"Well, James? I've given you until this evening to decide whether you will cease this absurd defiance, or ..."

"Be kicked out," Wrightson finished for him in a low voice. "You know quite well what the answer will be. I'm marrying Phyllis at the first opportunity, and if you can't approve, I'm sorry."

"Sorry!" Renway barked the words. "You'll be the biggest fool in creation if you insist. Give the slut up, and ..."

He realised before he had finished the sentence that he had gone too far. Wrightson's cheeks flamed, and he stood up, pushing his chair behind him sharply. It crashed to the floor, but neither man heeded it as their gaze met stormily.

"That's more than enough," Wrightson said, and his voice shook with suppressed anger. "I've stood a lot too much from you, and I'm through, do understand? Through. I've done my best to serve you, and I've tried to save you from making a fool of yourself over the Curtis woman. Now the quicker I'm away the better for us both."

Renway's lips tightened, but the Toff, had he been present, would have seen the anxiety in his eyes.

Outwardly, only his anger showed.

"An inheritance of a million isn't to be thrown away for nothing," he said stiffly.

"Nothing? I'd rather have Phyllis than all your filthy money!" The younger man's voice was harsh, strident. "Spend it on that doll who's following you around! Put your precious million into any crazy scheme you like, *I* don't want it!"

"No," said Renway, more slowly than before, "and certainly you won't get it. Before I leave you a penny piece I …"

He stopped suddenly, and as the younger man glared at him his face seemed to change colour.

Wrightson stepped forward quickly, putting an arm out to support his uncle; without it Renway would have fallen. For a moment they stood very still, with Renway breathing stertorously.

There was a bluish tinge to his lips that worried Wrightson. He knew his uncle's heart was not as strong as it might be, and, before the quarrel which had now been going on for weeks, he had been fond of the old man.

He led Renway to a chair, and poured out a little brandy. Renway gulped it down, still breathing hard. After a few seconds his colour grew more normal.

"That's—better! I–I thought I was going." The eyes of the two men met, and, surprisingly, Renway's thin hand went out and his fingers pulled Wrightson's sleeve. "James, don't make a hasty decision. I'm sorry if I said anything to offend you; temper is an ugly thing. Think things over well, my boy."

Wrightson's eyes were troubled, but unrelenting. He had no desire for the break, but he knew the choice had to be made eventually, doubted whether his uncle's attitude would alter; but the issue could be postponed.

"All right," he said. "We'll forget it for now, Uncle."

"Good!" said Renway. "Good! Now help me upstairs, there's a good fellow. I must go out tonight, and if I don't get a rest I'll be like nothing on earth. Old before my time, eh, Jimmy, and that won't do."

Wrightson did not say that the rest of the world believed his uncle to be ten years older than his age.

Chapter Nine

Of Phyllis

James Wrightson had a blank evening before him, and he did not feel like spending it at the St. John's Wood house. There had been times when he had been quite contented to browse among the classics, evenings which he had spent with his uncle and had enjoyed. The days for that were past, he knew, and he wondered how long it would be before the final break came.

Renway was with the Curtis woman, of course.

Wrightson, possessed of a sense of humour which had been sadly repressed of late, smiled crookedly at the thought of his uncle condemning Phyllis while being condemned for the Curtis woman. Irma had a beauty that Wrightson thoroughly disliked. The hothouse type, the siren-type; as different from Phyllis as the proverbial chalk from cheese.

It did not occur to him that he might be wrong. It did occur to him that Irma had been responsible in a large measure for the change which had come over his uncle, a change he did not consider was for the better.

There seemed nothing he could do to alter it.

He sat for a while in the study, which he had always shared with his uncle, brooding over the quarrel of that evening, and the heart attack which had followed. Such spasms were growing increasingly frequent, and Wrightson believed that the faster tempo of the life

Renway was leading with Irma Curtis – he knew nothing of her real name – was responsible for it.

Renway seemed quite blind to that possibility.

Renway, in fact, was an old man who had never married and who was 'seeing' a woman for the first time in his life. It was surprising that one of Irma's type had managed to snare him; he might have been expected to look for someone older, as company in his declining years.

Or might he?

Wrightson realised, if a little vaguely, that only Irma's startling looks could in the first place had attracted so confirmed a bachelor. She knew how to handle Renway, of course, and on the few occasions when she had met Wrightson she had been pleasantness itself. In short, he knew nothing specific about Irma to explain his acute dislike of her, and yet he knew that that dislike was in no small measure the reason for the trouble between himself and his uncle.

He was honest, too, when he claimed that he did not mind whether or not he inherited Renway's money. He had a few thousand pounds put aside, and he was experienced enough, and had enough friends, to get a reasonably well-salaried position in the City.

That would mean an income sufficient for Phyllis and himself.

He smiled as he thought of her, and wished that friends had not claimed her for the evening. She was somewhere in North London, and he did not even know the address. Odd, how lonely he felt when she was out of his reach.

After trying to read, he stood up from his chair, deciding to try to walk through the Parks to settle his mind. He did not make the experiment, however, for as he entered the hall there was a ring at the front door. He opened it, and in some surprise saw the immaculate figure of the man he had met that afternoon.

"I'm afraid Mr. Renway's out," he said.

"I'm not surprised," said the Toff. "I came to see you, Mr. Wrightson. I hope I'm not in the way."

Wrightson was intrigued, and in any case glad of the diversion. Rollison entered the house for the second time, and Wrightson found drinks – not Amontillado, but Johnnie Walker. Rollison chatted idly for a few minutes, for he wanted thoroughly to whet the other's curiosity. And he was succeeding.

He liked Wrightson even more at the second meeting than at the first. A clean-cut fellow, whose rugged good looks bespoke honesty as clearly as his blue eyes.

After thinking over the situation, the Toff had decided that a talk with him would be the next step in his plan of campaign, basing the decision on his assessment of Wrightson's character.

He opened the subject unexpectedly.

"I know it will seem an impertinence, Mr. Wrightson, but I came to see if you know much about the lady who is taking up so much of your uncle's time."

"No-o," said Wrightson, slowly.

He was inclined to be offended at first, however; he could think what he liked about his Uncle's friends, but certainly it was no business of other people's. Yet there was something about the Toff's smile that smoothed him down. "Isn't this rather an unusual opening gambit?"

"I won't say that I know for certain," said the Toff, who did not propose to commit himself on any point at that moment, "but I've an idea that she has been mixed up in some shady business in the past. She is – again I'm guessing – an adventuress of a rather different kind, and it seemed possible that you might be able to give me some idea of the kind of thing she might be able to wheedle out of you uncle. Does that make the gambit more understandable?"

He said it all lightly, but it shook Wrightson, who had considered nothing more than the usual association of rich man and loose woman with ambitions.

"It's still peculiar. What is your particular interest?"

"Purely that of an amateur," said Rollison cheerfully. "I have been known to look on when the police are working, and I know one or two of the rules. It struck me that if I could do anything to stop developments, you might like it. Provided developments are in the offing, of course. Kick me out if you want to," he added, with a smile. "Gently, of course!"

Wrightson did not kick him out.

For one thing, he suddenly remembered that he had seen the name of this man in Old Bailey trials; for another, he realised that a scandal of any kind would probably make his uncle's heart flutter for the last time. And, as the Toff had hoped, he liked the direct approach on a delicate subject.

He told all he knew and felt – that he disliked Irma, had warned his uncle against her, and would certainly watch any point that might arise. As far as Wrightson was aware, the only thing his uncle was planning was a new company, and Wrightson himself knew little about it. It was an electrical business, and executives from several large companies had promised to join the new one. Renway had kept everything quiet, wanting to put the new company on the market quickly and suddenly.

That, thought the Toff, was a considerable point. It might have been inspired by Irma, of course. On the other hand, it was a good business ruse, and there might be nothing questionable about it. He made no comment, and learned, among other things, of the trouble Renway had had with a man named Martin, an accountant who had worked for him for years. Martin was the only man apart from Renway himself to know a great deal about the old man's finances.

And then Wrightson mentioned Sidey – and the Toff knew he was getting very warm.

Sidey, Wrightson said, was an ex-convict who had been employed by Renway on Martin's introduction. Martin had been dismissed soon after Sidey.

Rollison already wondered whether there was a direct connection between Renway's ex-employees and Leopold Kohn.

Unfortunately Wrightson did not know where Martin lived, and the Toff would have to locate him. He did not think that likely to be difficult.

It was past nine when Rollison took his leave. Wrightson still felt puzzled, yet easier in his mind. Rollison, he recalled now, had a reputation to be envied; and if he was holding a watching brief, there was little or nothing to worry about.

It was an easy attitude, and a soothing one, for Wrightson's major concern was for the girl, Phyllis.

At twenty past nine the telephone rang. Wrightson answered it abruptly, and then his face brightened.

"Phyl, thanks be! How did you escape?"

"The party's postponed until tomorrow," said Phyllis Bailey cheerfully. "I've been dreadfully busy, darling, but I thought you might care to entertain me for an hour …"

"Where are you?"

"At Baker Street."

"Hop on a bus, darling, and come here. He's gone out …"

Renway was referred to as 'he' between them – "and we're all right for a couple of hours. I'll run you home in the car before zero hour. I've lots to talk about, including a visit from a man named Rollison, and his opinion of sweet Irma will make good hearing."

Phyllis laughed, promised to hurry, and rang off.

She arrived twenty minutes later, and Wrightson's earlier enthusiasm for the Rollison-Irma subject dimmed; they talked of more personal things, which was only to be expected.

He related the story of his quarrel with his uncle, and the end of it, and although she professed to be pleased, actually she was worried. The last thing she wanted to do was to cause a breach between Jim and his uncle, and little that had happened suggested that there would be a reconciliation while she remained engaged to him.

It had never occurred to Jim that she might break the engagement. It might not have occurred to her but for the fact that she knew Jim was worried, and hated the sight of his troubled face when ever – as now often happened – there had been words between him and Renway.

Phyllis had often wondered whether it would not be wiser for her to drop out of Wrightson's life. It depended, of course, on how much he really loved her. It was difficult to estimate, difficult to be sure whether he was in love with her or whether the opposition from Renway made his feelings seem more acute than in truth they were.

She was a small girl, yet not tiny, a brunette, and – as even the Toff would have agreed – very easy to look at. There was, in fact, a likeness between her and Anthea, although Anthea was so fair and Phyllis Bailey so dark. There was the same acute intelligence in grey eyes which were very steady, the same high brow, the same complete self-confidence. Her nose was short and the least bit *retroussé*, her lips were full and quick to smile. She sat back in an easy chair opposite Wrightson, completely self-controlled, graceful even while unmoving, nursing one knee in her hands and showing nice legs, and ankles which could hardly be more shapely.

She was a writer – not well known, though there was a circle of readers who enjoyed her books, which were neither fight romances nor heavy tragedies. She could capture the passing phases of modern life perfectly, and had a gift for characterisation which was the strength of her published work. A small independent income enabled her to write what she liked, as apart from what would earn the most money; and there were critics who prophesied for her a brilliant future.

The Toff would have liked her.

She looked on Wrightson rather in the same way as Anthea looked on her Jamie. He seemed incredibly young at times, at others older, far, than herself. There was so much about him to love: his directness, his honesty, his easy laughter, the warmth of his love for her. Still, she wondered whether it would be wise to allow this breach with Renway to worsen, wondered if he would be happy if she allowed it to.

She saw no way of healing it.

Thought of giving him up hurt: but other things in her life had been painful, and in his. If it would be the best thing for him, she could do it.

"Do you think he's dangerously ill, Jim?"

"We-ell, he is, of course. Anyone with a dicky heart ought to be careful, and he used to look after himself well enough. Fussed too much, as a matter of fact. Some doctor told him that he ought to get about more, and just then the Curtis woman arrived. He started stepping out, and of course nothing I can say now will make him see that he's asking for trouble."

"But if these attacks come more often he can't avoid seeing it."

Wrightson shrugged.

"You'd think so. But she's got such a hold on him that he just won't see what's under his nose. I think he would get up from his sick-bed to go out with her. Certainly he shouldn't have left his room tonight, to trot about the Embassy, with half London laughing at him," For a moment Wrightson looked and sounded bitter, but he went on in a few seconds with a light laugh: "We shouldn't grumble, at all events. The Fates work with us, my sweet – I get an evening free here, and you're let off! What happened to the party?"

"Big business or something equally tiresome."

"Hm. How's work?"

"I can't complain," said Phyllis. "I keep doing a little, and every day brings the new book nearer completion. One day I'll write a book worth writing, but now ..." She shrugged, and laughed. "It doesn't matter, Jim. What are *you* doing?"

He lifted his hands expressively.

"Hanging around. A dog's life, but I can't leave the old man as he is now, and he depends a lot more on me than he pretends."

"Ye-es," said Phyllis slowly.

Wrightson's expression showed surprise.

"Why do you speak like that, Phyl?"

Her grey eyes were sober.

"I don't like the way things are developing, Jim. He's set very firmly against me since he read some of my work – the Lord knows what he would think of the really modern writers if he calls mine indecent! and I don't want to force an issue."

Wrightson leaned forward and gripped her hand.

"Forget it, darling. You're not forcing an issue, he is. We mean too much to each other to look on it like that. If the true course won't run smooth ..." He shrugged; and in a few seconds he was sharing her chair – and Renway, the possibility of a broken engagement, work, worry and the Hon. Richard Rollison, were completely forgotten.

Rollison, meanwhile, had been summoned posthaste to Chamley Mansions, where Lady Munro greeted him with such warmth that he knew she had recovered from the aspersions which he had cast on Jamie. She gushed a little, allowed him to know that she was a devoted reader of thrillers, and assured him that to meet in real life a man who had figured as the central character in current novels was the thrill of the century.

The Toff made his escape to Anthea's room before her mother lapsed into the broad Americanisms of gangsterdom, to find Anthea looking thoroughly charming against the pillows, with a pink kimono about her shoulders. He pulled up a chair, and said severely:

"I'm not even going to shake hands with you, you incomparable charmer. If I do I shall forget myself and confess my love, and then what would poor Jamie do?"

"Fool! Rolly, I've discovered something about Wrightson and his girl."

"Good. Is she a Commie?"

"I wish you'd be serious. She writes."

"Well, that's no crime."

"Modern stuff," said Anthea. "Slightly advanced – but nice. I've been dipping into her latest – *Things We See* – and it's good, Rolly, it really is. I'd like to meet her. What kind of a man is this Renway?"

Rollison followed the trend of her mind.

"Very chaste, I imagine, where women are concerned. One of the old school, who considers the modern miss improper if she wears no stockings, and thinks toreador pants a creation of the Devil."

"That," said Anthea, "explains it. Phyllis Bailey's very modern— no dirt, Rolly, but definitely frank."

Rollison leaned forward, scanned a few pages of the book lying open on the bed, and then looked up thoughtfully.

"Certainly it explains Renway's dislike. I wonder if she's a beatnik or jeebies' chick, all wild parties and bad language."

"She isn't. Her people are *most* respectable, and she lives in Chelsea with them. She's rather sweet, I'm told."

"Who told you?"

"A friend who knows her."

"Hmm. Intelligence level?"

"High, apparently."

"Renway's opinion is different. Well, I'm bound to see something," said Rollison, "although I'm a long way from sure what it will be. You don't know anything more about Wrightson, do you?"

"Not a lot," said Anthea. "I found a girl who's fiancé knows him. He plays cricket and rugger, and got his cricket blue for Oxford five years ago. He doesn't do anything but help his uncle in his private business, and he's always been pretty fond of the old man. So far he hasn't shown anyone that he feels differently about him. He's quite crazy about Phyllis Bailey."

"He looked that way to me," said the Toff. "Anthea, you've been a big help, and thanks a million. Keep your ears and eyes open, and if you learn anything else that might be useful, phone me. Jolly can take a message if I'm out."

"What a funny-looking fellow he is, Rolly."

"Is he?" smiled the Toff. "He'd be delighted if he heard you say so, my pet, he thinks he always looks miserable. And now I'm off! Oh, when does the ankle begin to support you again?"

"Tomorrow," said Anthea firmly. "Doctor or no doctor."

"Sense or no sense," smiled the Toff. "All right, but it's on your own head if you have to go back to bed for a week. And what would your Jamie do then, poor thing?"

He went downstairs, dexterously escaping Lady Munro, knowing that the drawing-room door opened as the footman closed the front door behind him. He stepped into the darkness of Park Lane, pondering on Anthea's information, and finding that it was more of a hindrance than a help.

In one way, that was.

It was easy to understand why Renway would not countenance the engagement of his nephew to a women who wrote what he would consider 'advanced' literature. Or, more likely, 'obscene' literature. The library at the St. John's Wood house had proved that his taste was very innocuous, for none of the more advanced novelists had been included – there had been no Huxley, no Joyce, no Lawrence, only the steady, middle-of-the-road type of book, in which the characters were, for the most part, fully, even excessively, clad.

Renway was obviously stubborn too, and a man of set ideas.

The snag, as the Toff saw it, was that Anthea had located so sound a reason for Renway's opposition to the Wrightson-Bailey match, that it seemed unlikely that Irma was fanning the flames. The flames just would not need fanning. If that assumption were the right one, it cancelled the theory that Irma was trying to get Wrightson disinherited so that she would have more money when she married Renway.

If she married Renway.

Of one thing the Toff was certain. If she married him, he would not live long. Irma would not stand marriage to the old man; she would only contemplate it if he could be killed off, and his money pass into her hands.

The Toff had been rather fond of that theory, but now that it was weakened he thought more of the new electrical company that Renway was starting.

Wrightson could be believed, of course.

Moreover, Renway had assured Rollison that Bi-Nationals were perfectly good shares to hold. That might mean that Renway did not expect his new company to affect the Bi-National Corporation, or it might have been a move to cover up the indiscretion of his confidences in the Toff.

How far, in short, could Renway be trusted?

There were other questions.

Rollison wanted to get in touch with the man Martin, who might throw an interesting light on Sidey's activities. Martin had introduced Sidey to the millionaire, and then Sidey's true worth had been discovered, and both men had been fired. Rightly so. But thereafter, unless he was right off beam this time, Sidey had been murdered at Kohn's instigation.

Why should Kohn want Sidey dead?

Conceivably because he knew more than he should about the millionaire's new company, and on that assumption, Martin also knew something. Martin, then, was working with Kohn – and perhaps he too was in danger of his life.

"It doesn't clear up very much," the Toff admitted to himself, and he turned the wheel of his Frazer-Nash towards Gresham Terrace. To do so he had to make a sharp turn, and as he was concentrating on it, a car shot out of a turning opposite.

It happened as quickly as that.

The car had been without lights, and in the shadows. The Toff had not even seen that it was approaching, had not heard the engine until it accelerated sharply, rasping through the comparative silence of the night.

Rollison did the only thing he could, and trod heavily on the accelerator. Even then he wondered whether he would be in time; for a split-second it seemed that the other car would crash into him, striking the Frazer-Nash broadside. He knew fear in that split-second, a fear which was worse because there was little he could do.

And the the crash came.

The oncoming car struck the Frazer-Nash on the rear wheel, and the smaller car swivelled round, completely out of control. The Toff was jolted violently against the windscreen as the car reeled over to the right. He had been travelling at forty after the acceleration, and if he crashed it would mean serious injury at least.

He felt debris flying about him, and a piece struck the windscreen of the Frazer-Nash, dropping back after powdering the safety glass. The blow paralyzed him for a moment, made it impossible for him to regain control, while the car heeled over sickeningly.

Chapter Ten

Kohn Quickens the Pace

It was one of the worst moments of the Toff's life.

It would have been better had he been able to do anything at all, but to sit there with his mind active but his body helpless took him almost to the pitch of despair. He knew that the car had crashed into him deliberately, knew that this was another move on the part of Irma and Kohn, knew that he should have been expecting it. And in truth he had been prepared for an attack, but the way the other car had shot from the shadows had beaten him completely.

The Frazer-Nash struck something on the kerb, shuddered, and then very slowly sank back on all four wheels; the engine stalled.

There was a moment when the Toff was there alone, seeing what had happened. A street lamp, its light doused, had stopped the car from going over, but the standard itself was broken. It crashed down across the bonnet of the Frazer-Nash, and glass splintered about Rollison's head.

And then came footsteps, shouts of alarm, and the shrill blast of a policeman's whistle.

Rollison, for once in his life, was half-carried from the car, and he heard a man say gruffly:

"Lucky beggar—he ought to've been dead."

"Don't say such a thing, George!" A woman sounded shocked.

"I mean nine times out'a ten he would'a been. Wasn't his fault, I see what happened. The other car come across, and that lamp was out. Funny, that's what it looks to me."

Rollison was helped to the railings of a house, and he leaned against them thankfully, more stunned than hurt. He fumbled for his whisky flask; a swig, neat, did him good. A sensible policeman made no attempt to ask questions, but started a search for the driver of the other car, which had come off far more badly than the Toff's.

Someone offered Rollison a cigarette.

"Thanks," he said, and accepted a light. "All right, constable, I'm doing fine. Is the other poor chap hurt?"

The policeman had come back now that three others had responded to his whistle, and in the dim light from distant lamps he looked puzzled and perturbed.

"He's not there, sir."

The Toff stared.

"Not *there*?"

"No, sir. He must have jumped out when he saw it coming. Come and have a look for yourself."

The Toff accepted the invitation, and went towards the wreckage of the car which had crashed into him. Thirty or forty people had already gathered and dozens more were trailing up, to be moved on by the police. Rollison's mind was working fast again, and he knew the solution to this mystery before he saw the wreckage of the big car, which was unrecognizable, smashed to smithereens.

"Constable, I'd like to get away from here, straight to the Yard. Report this just as it's happened, and if you'll feel happier, send a man to the Yard with me."

The constable stared.

"I—oh, Mr. *Rolli*son." He touched his helmet, and made it clear that he did not consider it necessary for the Toff to go to the Yard under escort. Rollison left the fringe of the crowd and the policemen to the immediate problem of clearing the wreckage, and walked slowly – for he felt a little unsteady – towards Westminster.

Kohn, quite obviously, was quickening the pace.

There was no specific reason for going to the Yard, except that this crash must be reported to McNab, and it would look far better if he did it personally. There was, of course, a chance that McNab would not be at his office, but that hard-working officer proved to be at his desk, with a sergeant sitting at his side. He looked up when the Toff entered, and started.

"Rollison, what's the matter?"

"Matter?" asked the Toff, genuinely surprised.

"Your forehead, mon!" McNab pushed his chair back, while the Toff rubbed a hand across his forehead, to find that the blood from a cut had congealed. He realized that he must appear to be in a far worse state than he was.

McNab said abruptly: "All right, Wilson, we'll finish that tomorrow. Come along to the first-aid-room, Rollison."

A mirror showed Rollison that he looked a scarecrow, and certainly gave evidence of being in a rough-house. He washed, to find the cut not serious, although McNab insisted on dabbing iodine on it, and was only just prevented from using sticking-plaster. Brushed, his hair tidied, and his clothes smoothed down, Rollison felt much better. The effect of the smash was wearing off.

McNab's office was empty when they returned.

"Now, then, what is it?" demanded McNab.

"The truth, and nothing but the truth," said Rollison. "A simple enough matter, Mac. A lamp bulb or two had been removed to make the corner of Gresham Terrace dark, and a car was waiting for me on the other side of the road. The driver hurtled it at me, and jumped clear before he could suffer any harm. A good try, if an old one—the old tricks always come off best."

"Who was it?"

"I'm not a seer! But it's connected with the Sidey business, of course."

McNab settled back in his chair, and demanded to know just what the Toff had been up to. Rollison gave him a brief outline. He had no desire, yet, for the police to know too much – and he had sound reasons for that.

The police, of course, would tackle Benson directly that man was incriminated. They might also go for Kohn, and almost certainly they would question Irma if it were known she was in any way connected. To do that might stop the whole plot from maturing at once, but there was no definite evidence against Kohn or Irma, and Benson was only useful because he might lead the Toff to bigger things.

McNab listened, his chunky face expressionless, a pipe drooping from the corner of his thick lips. His light blue eyes stared unwaveringly at the Toff, who was in no way disconcerted.

McNab shrugged at last.

"This doesn't tell me enough, Rollison. You've been looking round friends of Sidey, you say, and—och, it's nonsense!" went on McNab, lapsing into broad Scots. "I'm not fule enough to believe ye've told me all there is to tellit, Rollison. Ye'll find one day ye'll be killit before ye've been wise an' come here with a full story."

"It will be a sad day," said the Toff sorrowfully, "but I'm hoping for the best. What have you been doing?"

The Chief Inspector lifted a stubby forefinger.

"Trying all I know, Rolleeson, with no results. Sidey's wife knows nothing, or pretends she doesn't. Sidey was running straight until he was dismissed from his job, and then it seems he fell back into his old ways. For the rest—there's nothing to be told."

"So you're no further ahead."

"Not an inch," said McNab.

"A pity," said the Toff, and then gently: "Sidey's wife—Minnie, isn't it? *Does* she know anything?"

"She insists that she doesn't."

"Hmm," said the Toff, and McNab made no further comment, which was in itself surprising, for it was virtually an invitation for the Toff to try to find out something from Minnie Sidey. It was obvious that McNab was completely puzzled, and that the police had so far unearthed nothing which would incriminate Kohn or lead to Irma.

The Toff was neither surprised nor sorry.

There would be time for the police later, and he would not delay it unnecessarily. But was keenly aware that precipitate action might lose him the day – and in spite of his caution, McNab could be precipitate.

The Toff returned to Gresham Terrace, pondering the Martin-Sidey-Minnie angle, and deciding that Minnie must be interviewed, and soon.

Not unnaturally, he considered that the Wrightson angle was, for the time being, the least important.

He was not to be blamed for that assumption. To all appearances it was a matter which concerned the private lives of Wrightson and Renway, and there appeared to be no sound reason for connecting it with the Irma-Renway tie-up. He did not dismiss the possibility that it was connected, of course, but certainly he would not have been surprised to learn that Irma was uninterested in Jim Wrightson.

Nor did he see any object in visiting Phyllis Bailey.

Anthea had, in fact, yielded more than he had expected in the way of assistance. His own talk with Wrightson had been informative, but Wrightson was the type of youngster who would get on his high horse quickly if he learned that his Phyllis was being questioned. He had enough on his mind as it was, and the Toff went to bed early, prepared for a day in the East End on the morrow, to find – if it were findable – what he could about the part Charlie Wray had played in this affair.

Which was not likely to be welcomed by Wray.

And which did nothing to help Phyllis Bailey, although she had no idea that she needed help. Despite the interlude with Jim Wrightson on the previous night, she had found herself that day convinced that the engagement was doing him more harm than good. She had convinced herself that he hated the thought of a break with his uncle, a break inevitable while she was engaged to him.

The bridge-party on the following night found her inattentive, and unpopular with her partner. She missed a Grand Slam which a beginner would have called, at a moment when she was wondering whether to tell Jim, to telephone him, or to write to him.

Renway had made it clear not only that he considered her a scheming hussy, but that she would do his nephew considerable harm if she persisted in the engagement. That night, particularly, she was more concerned because she knew it was zero hour. The old man would either withdraw his objections, or the break would come.

If it did come?

She was robbing Jim of his prospects, standing in his way and doing a lot more harm than she could possibly do good. If she made a firm stand on the following evening – provided Paul Renway had maintained his objections – she would have much more self-respect. It would at least serve to prove just how much Jim cared.

Had she been honest with herself she would have admitted that was her chief concern.

The prospect was not a cheerful one, and she disliked the long bus ride back to Chelsea, since it allowed her to dwell on the situation. When at last she reached the bus stop she hurried along Dray Street – in the better residential part of Chelsea – anxious to get home, and find someone to talk to.

She would not have noticed the men who were waiting opposite the house had they not stepped forward. She started; it was dark here, and she could see little more than their outline.

"Excuse me, Miss ..."

"I beg your pardon?" Phyllis sounded stiff.

"I hope I haven't startled you." The shorter of the two men was speaking, his voice suave. "Are you Miss Bailey—Miss Phyllis Bailey?"

"I am." Her thoughts flew immediately to Jim. "Is there something the matter?"

"Nothing serious." The speaker smiled, and his expression was pleasant enough. "Mr. Wrightson ..."

So it was Jim. Her eyes narrowed, and she waited tensely for the man to go on. In that moment she realized more than ever before how much Jim mattered.

"A slight accident in his car," said the shorter man, easily. "Nothing to worry about, I assure you, but he would like to see you at the St. John's Wood house. If you are free, of course."

"I'll go at once." She started to turn back to the main road. "No need to worry about buses," said the stranger. "Jim asked me to come and collect you." He pointed to the car on the other side of the road. "We'll be there in twenty minutes." There was something in his smile that she did not like, and on the spur of the moment she said: "I'll have to slip in and tell my mother."

As she spoke there was a queer impression in her mind that all was not as it should be. She knew few of Jim's friends, and from the short man's mention of his name it seemed he was a friend – but this was hardly the way Jim would have sent for her. And why had *two* men been waiting?

The speaker's next words came quickly.

"It won't help, I'm afraid. We've knocked several times, but had no answer."

Phyllis frowned, for she had had no idea that her family would be out. She excused herself and unlocked the door with her key. There was no one in, and she left a brief note: *I'll be back late.*

That was enough to prevent her parents from worrying. "All clear?" asked the man smoothly as she reappeared. "Will you sit in the front with me, or do you prefer the back?" "The back, please." "Right-ho! Hop in!"

Phyllis obeyed, and a few seconds later the car, a modern streamlined Austin, moved silently from the kerb. She was more worried than she showed; a slight mishap might mean anything, and Jim would not alarm her unnecessarily. At least, he was at his home and not at a hospital, a reassuring thought.

It was warm in the car.

It grew warmer, and she felt tired. Her head dropped once or twice, and she closed her eyes, only to force herself awake again quickly and look round, uncertain where she was. The third time she did not open her eyes, and her breathing grew very soft and regular.

The car did not go to St. John's Wood, but took the main Essex road.

At a junction of the road across Epping Forest the Austin stopped and the smooth-voiced driver – none other than 'Ritzy' Martin – stepped out. The road was deserted, but even had a dozen people passed they would have thought it nothing but thoughtfulness to tuck the rug round the knees of the sleeping girl.

He jumped back into his seat and slammed the door.

"She's all right," he said. "Sweet dreams until the morning and then a thick head. After that—well, we don't have to worry."

"Ask Mr. Ruddy K.," grunted the taller man, whose voice was a long way from pleasant, and would have aroused Phyllis's suspicions had she heard it. It was harsh, ill-educated, and certainly not that of a man whom Jim Wrightson was likely to call a friend.

The run to Epping had been made to ensure that no one had followed, and they turned back, eventually reaching a house in Leaning Street, Aldgate.

The man who opened the door was known as Mr. Brown. He was mufflered up as he usually was, but his glasses were missing, for Ritzy and the other man knew him as Kohn as well as Brown, wherein they had an advantage over Benson.

"You've got her?" said Kohn, and Ritzy laughed.

"She'll be round in the morning." He was smiling; a disarmingly attractive man, Ritzy Martin nearly always created a good impression. "All ready for you, Boss."

"Tomorrow's too late," said Kohn.

It was difficult to rouse the girl, but it had to be done, for Kohn was not a man to argue with. Some twenty minutes after she had entered the house she opened her eyes. Her head was throbbing, and her throat was sore, but otherwise she felt no ill-effects of the drug which she had breathed in the car. She managed to struggle to her feet from the settee on which she was lying, and as she did so she saw the dark eyes of Leopold Kohn.

Something in them frightened her.

"You and I are going to talk," said Kohn. His voice was cold, and the girl flinched.

She said: "This is outrageous. I ..."

Kohn leaned forward and brought the palm of his hand across her face. It was abrupt, brutal, entirely unexpected. She swayed backwards, and the red mark of his hand showed clearly on her cheek. Her eyes were narrow, but there was stubbornness and spirit as well as fear in them.

"Speak when I tell you," said Kohn. "You visited Paul Renway's home last night."

"And if I did ..."

"Don't talk back!" His lips tightened as he struck her again, and she nearly lost her balance. "Just do as you're told. You talked with Wrightson, your fiancé. He had been visited by a man named Rollison earlier in the evening, and he probably talked to you about it."

"I—had no idea." She lied, and intended to lie, although she was cold with a fear of things she did not understand.

"You'll remember differently," said Kohn.

He struck her again until her head was burning and tears filled her eyes, but not until the glowing end of a cigarette touched her arm did she give way. It was unbearable, an incredible thing, but she knew this man would go to any lengths of persuasion; lying served no further purpose.

Kohn listened to her recital, his lips still taut, until he knew just what Wrightson had told her of his conversation with Rollison. The girl was half-fainting when she had finished; in an hour she seemed to have aged years.

Kohn had interrogated her alone; now he touched a bell, and the taller of her captors entered.

"Put her to sleep," Kohn said. "I shan't want her again."

There was real terror in Phyllis Bailey's eyes as the roughneck pressed a pad over her mouth, and the sickly smell from it went through her nostrils and she felt her senses going. She tried to struggle, but she was powerless; her last conscious thought was that she might never wake up again. The abruptness of it all had a nightmarish horror.

Kohn laughed as the man, Billy to his friends, carried her out as effortlessly as he would a child.

Ten minutes later Kohn left the Leaning Street house and returned to the flat at Arch Mansions. The flat was empty and it was later before Irma returned, later still when he had finished what he had to tell her. She was smoking a cigarette in a long holder, and her eyes were narrowed as she listened. At last: "So Rollison knows about as much as we thought he did, and nothing more. Is it worth keeping the girl?"

"For the time being, yes," said Kohn. "Wrightson will have to be brought in, or he will make a nuisance of himself, which would not do. Afterwards" – he smiled thinly and shrugged his shoulders – "we will do what is most convenient. She would not recognize me—although she might remember Mr. Brown – and Wrightson will not see me. But we will not pronounce a verdict yet, my dear, we will wait on events."

Irma smiled at him through a haze of smoke, although she knew the verdict he spoke of would be one of life or death. That mattered less than the fact that he was demonstrating a ruthless efficiency likely to make the Toff think hard.

"It sounds all right, Leo. But don't take what you've learned about Rollison at its face value. He's smarter than you realize."

"I think," said Kohn softly, "that you are at once inclined to overrate Rollison and to underrate me, my dear. We have been co-operating for a long time. Have you ever known me make a serious error?"

"No-o," said Irma as softly. "But you've never met Rollison before. He's not easy, Leo. How many attempts have we made on his life? Three, including that fool Wray's attempt to run him down in Aldgate. He's got away without any trouble each time, and he's sent you one of those visiting cards to mock you."

Kohn shrugged. He was looking more self-satisfied than when he had received the Toff's card, for he had had time to tell himself that he was being unnecessarily worried, and that Rollison was endeavouring to use a bluff as a weapon. His pale face and somewhat ascetic looking expression, were not those of a man utterly devoid of scruple, with many murders on his conscience. It seemed incredible that he was the same mufflered and disguised "Mr. Brown" who had tortured Phyllis Bailey.

"I am really not alarmed, my dear. Rollison escaped tonight, but he will by now be worried. Very worried, unless I'm considerably mistaken. And there will come a time when his luck will fail him."

"I wonder," said Irma. She stood up abruptly and stepped to the window, looking out into the street below. "I've an unpleasant feeling that he knows more than we think, Leo. You haven't known him after you before; you don't know what he's like. As for worrying him—that's nonsense. Nothing ever does. And it's easy to call it luck, but he gets away with it so often that there must be some other explanation. He's uncanny, and" – she shivered, although the room was warm – "I wish it was over."

"You're losing your nerve," said Kohn softly. "That won't do, my dear."

"It's this continual waiting—it's always worse when he's doing nothing, or when we think he's doing nothing."

Kohn said quietly: "He thinks he's doing something. He just doesn't know where to start. We'll have Wrightson safe before tomorrow's out, and after that Rollison will be helpless. Wrightson might have picked up information that could be damaging; it's not safe to leave him loose. Get to bed, my dear. Don't worry about anything except doing what I tell you, and doing it quickly."

She stared at him, and there was a touch of annoyance in her manner.

"I think you said I co-operate, Leo. Don't forget that's the basis we work on. I don't take orders."

For a moment it looked as if he was going to force an issue, and his eyes were hard. She out-stared him, the smoke curling from her lips, one hand at her waist. There was insolence, and a challenge in her manner, and the Toff would have been delighted had he seen this evidence of a coming quarrel among thieves.

The tension broke.

"Of course, of course," said Kohn. "We're both a little on edge, my dear, that's all. I ..."

And then he stopped, and she swung round towards the door, for the front bell rang sharply. Kohn slipped his right hand into his pocket as he stepped towards it, evidence of his nerves being in bad shape despite his words. But there was no one outside when he looked on to the landing.

There was something on the door.

A card, one of the Toff's, with the absurd little drawings at their rakish angle, and in ink the words: *"We won't be long now, will we, Leo?"*

Chapter Eleven

Rumours of Hush-Hush

It was a remarkable fact that the Toff contrived to arrange the arrival of his cards to coincide with the exact moments they would have the most effect. He called it luck, although in truth it was his remarkable ability to judge the psychological moment.

That night he had sent his card – via Jolly – as an acknowledgment of the latest attempt to kill him, while among other things he had done before retiring was to arrange with his garage for the provision of another Frazer-Nash until his own was in running order again.

He felt satisfied, up to a point.

Had he known anything of the disaster which had overtaken Phyllis Bailey, he would not, however, have been so satisfied with himself.

Phyllis's parents were worried when she did not come down to breakfast the next morning, but a telephone call purporting to come from a friend set their minds at rest. Phyllis worked in a study which she shared with a friend, and occasionally spent the night there.

Wrightson might have been worried, but he knew she was busy and was not really surprised when she did not ring him that morning. He wondered whether she had enjoyed her evening, and he was still wondering when the telephone-bell rang at last. It was after dark, and he had contemplated going out.

A strange voice greeted him and some twenty seconds later he was told that Phyllis had fallen down a flight of stairs and twisted her ankle. Would he go to see her? She was with friends at 28 Abbott Road, Highgate.

"I'll be there in half an hour," said Wrightson promptly.

It was an optimistic claim, but he was in his car within five minutes of getting the message and speeding towards Highgate. The accident sounded trivial, but Phyllis was not likely to send a message to alarm him, and probably when he found her he would discover the injuries much worse. He was even prepared to find them disastrous. Luck, and two policemen who failed to see his number, enabled him to reach Highgate without trouble, and he was knocking on the door of 28 Abbott Road just inside his time limit.

It was one of a hundred terrace houses, all of which were of the same, drab grey and he told himself that it was one of the most distressing suburban streets he had been in for a long time. He even wondered what Phyllis had been doing there.

There was no immediate reply to his knock, and the silence and the gloom inside the house irritated him. He knocked again, and a moment later a light was switched on in the hall. The door opened and a thick-set, florid-faced man with a heavy moustache peered at him. His voice was that of the man who had telephoned, although now it seemed harsher and less educated.

"Mr. Wrightson? I'm glad yer've come. Come in, do."

Wrightson stepped through.

"How is she?"

He did not see the expression on the man's face, for Jake Benson was behind him, closing the door. It was a leer; and would have warned Jim Wrightson of impending trouble.

"Not so bad, mister, not so bad. She's upstairs."

Wrightson frowned, but started upstairs quickly. There was no light in the house apart from the hall, and no sound but the footsteps of the two men. Wrightson was puzzled, for it was an unlikely place for Phyllis to come to; and he had not liked the look of the man.

"In here," said Benson.

He switched on a landing-light and opened a door. Wrightson stepped into the room, and found himself looking at a few empty chairs, a deal table and half a dozen wall texts of the hell-fire variety. He swung round quickly, his eyes alarmed.

"What the devil's this? ..."

It was not until then that he saw the gun in Benson's hand.

For a moment he was too stupefied to act or think, and before he had recovered himself Benson drove a fist viciously into the pit of his stomach. Wrightson groaned and doubled up, and the butt of the revolver cracked on his head, a roaring filled his ears.

He dropped heavily.

He was still unconscious when Benson and Ritzy took him from Abbott Road to Leeming Street, by car, and although he could not know it, locked him in the room next to Phylfis Bailey's.

Leopold Kohn was having an easy run.

The Toff knew nothing of these things when they occurred.

He saw no reason at all to suspect that Wrightson or his girl was in any danger, but he did believe Renway was likely to run into trouble before long. He was particularly anxious to keep an eye on the man, and for the time being concentrated on that.

Consequently he was at the So-So Club on the night after Phyllis Bailey had been kidnapped, and about the time that Jim Wrightson was being knocked out.

Irma had her fiancé were at the Club. The Toff had followed Renway from the Park Terrace house earlier in the evening and seen him collect Irma from the Marble Arch flat. They had dined at the Embassy at a table where he could see them and they could see him, but as he was with a lady of uncertain reputation even Irma was prepared to believe him to be on pleasure bent. At ten o'clock they left for the So-So, and by then the Tuff was bored with his companion. She left him, disappointed and angry.

The So-So was a night club typical of a dozen others, and he had long since exhausted all the interest they had for him. The clientele was mainly composed of youngsters hardly breeched and old folk like Renway with more money than sense. The Toff did not dance, although many hopeful glances were sent towards him, and he wondered whether it was worth while waiting. The So-So Club was above reproach; Irma and Renway were there simply for pleasure, and the only satisfaction to be derived was the knowledge that Irma knew he was there simply to watch her.

It was one o'clock, ahead of his quarries, left the Club.

He did not think he was observed as he guided the nose of his hired Frazer-Nash some fifty feet behind their taxi. The cab took a long route to Arch Mansions, where Irma got out. Renway did not go up to her flat, possibly a significant fact, suggesting that Irma was holding him at arm's length.

The Toff could see no benefit likely to come from visiting Irma or Kohn again that night, and he certainly had no desire to follow Paul Renway home. Had he done so, he might have been saved the shock which came next morning, but he was not to know that – for he was not ominiscient despite rumours to the contrary. He turned the nose of his Frazer-Nash to Gresham Terrace, yawning several times on the short run home.

Chief Inspector McNab had held hopes of getting to bed towards midnight, but he had been called out on an urgent job, and in consequence it had been nearly 1 a.m. before he reached the Yard again. There he found a report from the plain-clothes men watching Minnie Sidey, and the report made him wrinkle his broad nose.

He telephoned Rollison, to find that Jolly was "expecting Mr. Rollison at any time". McNab was nothing if not persevering, and he walked to the Toff's flat, arriving there some five minutes before the Toff. The latter's surprise was gratifying, and McNab said the obvious.

"Ye didn't expect me, Rollison."

"I did not," said the Toff. "But it's always a pleasure to talk to the most shining light of the Yard. Have a drink and do put that cigarette out, old boy, it's foul. How long have you had it in your pocket?"

"It's one of your own," said McNab, glancing towards a box on the table.

"Well, well, well," murmured the Toff, "and I thought you were an honest man." He dispensed whisky and soda, and sat back elegantly in an easy chair. "And now let it come."

"It's the Sidey business, Rollison."

"Really?" said the Toff.

"You know he was married," McNab said, pushing a hand through his sandy hair.

"We did talk about it, I fancy."

"Have you seen his widow?"

"Certainly not," said the Toff, and for a moment he was afraid of learning news which would make him wish that he had.

"The thing is," went on McNab, "my men think she's aware they're on her tail, and she won't move anywhere. I was wondering if you could watch her for a day or two? She'll not get on to you as she would my men, and I've an uncomfortable feeling she knows things she won't talk about."

It was the nearest thing to a compliment that McNab had ever paid him, and the Toff was surprised. He thought quickly. Even had there been no connection between the murder of Sidey and the Irma-Kohn-Renway business he would have been interested. There was, however, a possibility that he would learn something very worth while. In any case his call on Minnie was overdue.

Consequently he nodded.

"Good man," said McNab. "You'll tell me if you find anything, of course."

"Of course," said the Toff reproachfully. "Have your bloodhounds off in the morning, and I'll be along before the lady gets around."

McNab departed, well satisfied, for he knew the Toff could be relied on to allow a full meed of credit to fall on his shoulders, while the Toff smoked a final cigarette and wondered whether there was any ulterior motive in McNab's unexpected call. A visit so late at night certainly suggested that McNab was anxious indeed to get Rollison working. In the second, it was normally not McNab's policy to invite assistance, but rather to grumble and protest when that assistance was offered. The call, therefore, had two things which were peculiar, and to the Toff it suggested only one thing.

The police were stumped on the Sidey murder, and McNab was being pressured by the Assistant Commissioner to get results.

It had its humours, particularly since the Toff could have placed a finger on Benson at any time, with reasonable evidence to get him convicted. But as a whole there was little to laugh about in a case which the Toff was beginning to find exasperating. Despite the attacks on him, there was not a tittle of evidence to show what Kohn was after.

Rollison had made considerable efforts during the day to trace the man Martin. All he had discovered so far was that he was called 'Ritzy' by his friends, that he had a bad reputation, that he was a clever accountant, and had not been in the hands of the police. Because of that last fact he was, presumably, considered a law-abiding citizen. Such assumption was not fully justified, as the Toff knew well. But it was always difficult to work against a man who had no past record. The reason for that was simple: there was no easy way of finding his weaker points.

He needed to talk to Ritzy Martin.

He had visited the Blue Dog earlier in the evening, to find Charlie Wray as enormous, as smiling, as smooth and as dangerous as ever. Benson had been in the bar for a quarter of an hour, and had then gone to the private parlour upstairs. Thither Charlie had followed him, two others had joined them, and the Toff had heard nothing to assist him, except a stream of bad language from Benson, for whom the cards – they were playing solo – did not run well.

The card game suggested that nothing was likely to happen immediately.

The Toff, returning to Gresham Terrace, had found Jolly back with a similar report. Jolly had visited the three addresses where Ritzy Martin had been known to live, but the man had not been at any of them and none of his landladies had any idea where he was. The fact that they had not complained of rent owing was reasonable evidence that he had kept his accounts with them clear. He did not, therefore, shift from one place to another because he found it cheaper, but because he wanted to.

In all likelihood, the Toff considered, the unknown person in the Kohn case kept switching his living-quarters because he wanted to make it difficult to be traced.

"We could ask Kohn," the Toff had commented, and Jolly had grunted in a manner suggesting that he did not approve of such levity.

Afterwards, with hindsight, he knew that he should have suspected that there would be trouble for both Wrightson and Phyllis Bailey. True, there was no positive reason for his thinking that way, but he was so completely surprised by that development, so utterly deceived, that it remained a sore point with him for a long time.

He was surprised, he said, that he had slept in any degree of comfort that night, appalled when he learned that within three miles of him, Phyllis Bailey was lying half-asleep and half-unconscious, herself appalled by the brutality of the man whom she had heard called Brown.

The bruises of Kohn's blows were still on her cheeks, she had eaten little, and had only water to drink. In her eyes there was an expression akin to horror – an expression caused by the utter stupefaction which she had felt at the kidnapping and the brutality of her captor.

Why had Brown been interested in the man Rollison?

Why had it been necessary to kidnap her?

How was Jim in danger – if at all?

Would she ever go free?

These thoughts, preying on her mind, were made more fearsome by the effect of the drug which had been pumped into her. She had been torn out of her usual quiet, serene life, her emotional worries over Jim had been suddenly thrust into the background. If anything had evolved from it, it was realization of the depth of her love for Jim – who, she felt, was in danger as great as hers.

She was hungry, her face was bruised and painful, and she was afraid.

She did not know whether she would be alive on the morrow.

Wrightson, in the room next to her, was in little better shape.

He had not been questioned, but had been struck a dozen times by Benson, and later by a smooth-voiced, flashily handsome man whom he had heard called 'Ritzy'. All the time that he had seen Ritzy it had been in semi-darkness, and he had not recognized the accountant who had admitted Sidey into his uncle's office. He should have recognized him, but like his fiancée, he was too startled by the developments, torn so abruptly from his usual life that the only thing which occurred to him was to try to think *why*?

And, of course, he thought of Irma, and the Toff's warning.

He was afraid, too, for Phyllis.

The fact that she had been used as a bait to get him to the Highgate house was preying on his mind. He could see no reason why she should be in danger, and yet he felt that she was. The uncertainty of it was the thing that worried him most, although he would have been in no better shape had he known that only a breeze block partition separated her from him.

His helplessness, the chafing of the cords at his wrists, the suddenness of the attack, all combined to infuriate and to prevent him from retaining a balanced judgment. He was liable to do any crazy thing if the opportunity arose, and – although he did not know it – he was very close to death.

Meanwhile, Leopold Kohn, considering every angle of the campaign which he was conducting, felt that there was nothing likely to upset his arrangements. A few hours was sufficient for him to recover from the effect of the Toff's cards – although subconsciously he was on edge, and without fully realizing it he pondered each move more carefully than he would have done had he not known the Toff was watching.

Still, Kohn considered his moves were foolproof, and he did not feel that there would be acute danger. The only people who might threaten his security were either in his employ, or captive: and in either case could be killed and thus made safe at very short notice.

And the events of that night, then unknown to the Toff, would help Kohn considerably.

Chapter Twelve

Sensation!

The Toff awakened next morning with a clear head and an easy conscience, but a feeling that all was not right with the world. So far as he knew, there was not the slightest reason why he should have that feeling, and after he had pressed the bell for Jolly to bring his tea he lit a cigarette and browsed, going through the events of the previous day.

The main point had been McNab's call.

Nothing else had been outstanding – but, on the other hand, there had been no major setbacks, and if results were slow in coming, that was no reason for him to assume that they would not come.

For some quite obscure reason he found himself wishing that he had been to see Phyllis Bailey.

"Which," he assured himself, "is absurd. She plays no part in this. You're getting to a period of wishful thinking, and that won't help you or anyone. Come in, Jolly."

Jolly entered, with the tea and papers.

The Toff read a variety of papers, from the stately *Times* to the yellowest of the yellow Press, and confessed a complete distrust of them all. He opened the *Morning Wire* and then sat up abruptly in bed, more startled than he had been for years. For the *Wire*, to his astonishment, showed a photograph of James Wrightson and a girl who, despite the offences of the blockmakers, looked charming.

The Toff stared at them for a full thirty seconds without reading the headlines, and then drank his tea with some deliberation.

Jolly, whom the Toff sometimes called the most inquisitive man on earth, ventured a question: "No disturbing news, sir, I trust?"

"So do I," said the Toff. He eyed the lean and dyspeptic-looking manservant with disfavour. "Jolly, I'm going to be busy, and I want my breakfast in a hurry."

Jolly turned to obey, understanding that it was no time for talk, and the Toff read the story.

It could not be said that he was wholly surprised, for he had had an inkling a day or two before; but he was startled. He had certainly not expected it to come so quickly, and he was surprised that even the *Morning Wire*, supreme among sensational dailies, considered Wrightson a big enough subject for a headline and front-page photograph.

The story, by-lined with the name of a popular columnist, read:

MILLIONAIRE'S HEIR ELOPES
DEFIES GUARDIAN'S BAN

After the runaway heiresses ... a runaway heir.

Last night I talked with Mr. Paul Renway, distinguished art critic – *oh! thought the Toff* – and financier, who recently retired from the Boards of several big companies. He confirmed that his nephew, Mr. James Wrightson, had defied his objections to a marriage with Miss Phyllis Bailey, the well-known authoress, and eloped. A note explaining what he had done and why ...

The Toff read the rest quickly. Although he was interested in a fatherly way in Jim Wrightson's high handed burning of boats it was, after all, what could be expected from that headstrong-looking youngster – he was much more interested in the last paragraph, since it appeared to touch the affair itself more closely.

I also understand that Mr. Renway's interest in the City is not dead. There are rumours of plans for the formation of a new company. He would not comment on these rumours, but ...

The Toff gave a great deal of thought both to that and to the statement that Wrightson and the girl had eloped. He read an interview with Mrs. Bailey, who had been worried the first night her daughter had not turned up at home, but had received reassuring news the next day. Mrs. Bailey claimed she was quite happy to trust Jim Wrightson, whom she knew slightly.

Neither the Toff nor Mrs. Bailey realized her "reassuring news" had been faked.

The Toff concentrated finally on the cleverness of the final paragraph. Renway's new company would get more publicity from this than from all the City pages put together.

He did not know Renway well, but he doubted whether the man was capable of so astute a move; he wondered whether Irma or Kohn was behind the announcement: certainly it was typical of Irma. The City would be interested, and when the new company came into being it would not be a complete surprise. With Renway's name behind it, it would carry weight and with Kohn and Irma mixed up in it, it would almost certainly be one of the biggest frauds of the year. The thing was to prove it. The Toff had given up looking for other motives; the company was undoubtedly involved.

He felt perturbed, for there was no direct line that he could see, and he told himself that it was certainly past time that he saw Minnie Sidey; that seemed the only loophole in the game Irma and Kohn were playing, since Ritzy Martin was so shy.

It was eleven o'clock that morning that Minnie Sidey heard the telephone-bell ring in her flat. She answered it to recognize Jake Benson's voice.

"What's doin' this mornin'?"

"No sign of no one," said Minnie, with some relief. "I reckon it would be all right. But listen, Benson, I'm leaving a note saying where I'm going *and* who I'm going to see. No funny stuff, got me?"

Benson chuckled hoarsely.

"Careful, duckie. Don't you worry. I'll see you get a square deal. I wouldn't serve you brown fer a mint o' money. All square, see?"

"Like Alf, eh?"

"'E wasn't no use to you or no one. Stop worrying abaht 'im. All right for dibs, aincha?"

"I'm not grumblin' about that," said Minnie tartly, "but I know you tykes. I'll come to Sam's for dinner. Sam's is safe, and I c'n trust him."

"Sams'll do me fine," said Benson. "Toodle-oo, duckie."

He rang down, and made a comment to himself about the red-headed she-cat in language which Minnie would gladly have matched, for she distrusted Benson and all for whom Benson worked. But she had no alternative in the present circumstances but to do what he said: which did not make the situation easier for her, nor less worrying.

The dicks had been on her doorstep too long.

They were missing that morning, and Minnie – who at heart was a simple soul if not an innocent one – assumed that McNab had at last decided that there was nothing she could tell him about Sidey's death. She had put one over him nicely. Not that it hadn't been a shock, but …

The door of her sitting-room opened abruptly.

Minnie was wearing only a pair of slacks, and a brassiere. The latter was not wholly necessary for her thin chest, but she had her sense of modesty. She had been about to wash when the telephone call had come. Now she looked, startled and momentarily afraid, at a pair of trousered legs which showed at the door, and the hand that came through.

She exclaimed aloud as she made a dive for the bathroom.

When the door opened more widely and the Toff stepped through, immaculate in a navy blue lounge suit with a gardenia in his button-hole, she was standing by the half-open bathroom door with a towel held in front of her. The Toff saw her freckled face, and sensed something of the fear which was in her. That in itself was a point of considerable interest, and suggested that McNab had been right in his suspicions.

Minnie would not be scared unless there was good reason.

He closed the door behind him, and took out cigarettes.

"Come on now, Minnie, don't be shy. No one's going to hurt you."

Minnie's green eyes blazed.

"Why, you …"

"Easy, easy," said the Toff, "early morning's no time for it, sweetheart, and I don't like bad language from ladies, it never seems to run true. Clothe yourself, and come and talk with me."

He knew that he had her worried; which was why he had let himself in, using a picklock so silently that she had not heard him manoeuvring it at the door. She knew him, of course, although not well – they had not previously done business together.

Minnie's red hair was tousled, but held together with a green bandeau which made her forehead seem higher and shinier than it was. There was both fear and hate in her eyes as she regarded the Toff and stepped forward, the towel about her shoulders. The Toff was amused when she stepped to the mantlepiece, took a pin from a cushion there, and ostentatiously pinned the towel around her. Then she stepped to the table and put both hands on it.

Her language was not nice, and she treated the Toff to a three-minute peroration. She was a little breathless when she finished, while the Toff's smile remained unaltered.

"Nice to know, that you've such a vocabulary, my dear," he said. "I was prepared to be sorry for you, but I'll withdraw such unnecessary emotion. Minnie, you're in bad with the police."

She flinched, but her tongue was quick.

"I don't give a damn fer them blasted narks, see? Nor fer you, Mr. Ruddy Rollison. Clear out, and don't come back. I reckon you know more about Sidey than anyone, you …"

"Still lurid?" asked the Toff, but his voice was sharper. "That's enough, Minnie. You're in bad with the police, and you're mixing up with the crowd that killed Sidey. They'll kill you as cheerfully as they did him. You're dangerous to them, Minnie, and he was dangerous to them. That's why he died."

Her breathing was sharper.

"Get out, you liar!"

"You've just once chance," went on the Toff. "And that's to come clean. You daren't tell the police, but you can tell me, and I'll look after you. Who was Sidey working with when he died?"

"I don't know," snarled Minnie, "and if I did I'd cut my throat before I let a squeak out to you, Rollison! Clear out, and make it quick. Sidey was on the up-and-up, anyway, and ..."

"Sidey was killed by the same people who will kill you," insisted the Toff very softly, "and I can keep you out of it, Minnie. No one else can. Be sensible, and talk."

He stopped, and he waited, seeing the doubt in her eyes and wondering whether she would break down, or whether she could brazen it out. She knew that Sidey had been working with Benson and others, that was obvious. What mattered was whether her fear of the Benson gang would be greater than her fear of the Toff, and he believed he could throw a scare into her before he left which would bring the whole story.

And then, sharply, the telephone rang.

They had been staring at each other, the Toff's eyes cold and accusing, Minnie's hot and worried. Now they both looked sharply away towards the telephone, and Minnie took a short step forward. The Toff lifted a hand, and she stopped immediately. He strolled to the table where the telephone was standing, and lifted the instrument without moving his eyes from her.

"Yes?" He altered the timbre of his voice, and he did not sound like the Toff. The answering voice was feminine, and it was high-pitched; it also sounded puzzled.

"Is that Mrs. Sidey's flat?"

"Yes," said the Toff, and he handed the telephone towards Minnie. Through his mind flashed the likelihood that whoever was calling her would assume that she was forgetting Sidey quickly.

He would have been more concerned had he heard the man who spoke to Minnie Sidey.

He did not blame himself afterwards, for it had been cleverly done. There were more people who could change their voices in London than he liked to count – and Irma Cardew had changed hers then.

Minnie recognized Irma's real voice, had heard it time enough when Irma had talked to Sidey. The only sign that she gave was a slight tightening of her knuckles as she "gripped the telephone, while the Toff watched her, frowning a little, wondering whether he should have let her take the call."

It was done.

"Rollison's with you," said Irma very softly. "If you let out a squeal, Minnie, you'll go where your husband did. Send him out at once. Follow?"

"Yeah—sure." Minnie did it perfectly, the off-handed words, the careless Americanisms. It was how she would have talked to anyone, and it relieved the Toff of his feeling that he had made a mistake.

"Be quick about it," said Irma. "The flat's watched; if he's not out in two minutes you're for the high jump."

She rang down abruptly, and the Toff heard the click of the instrument at the other end. Minnie replaced hers slowly, and in her eyes was fear – but not the fear which the Toff had wanted to see, not fear of him.

He knew, then, that he had been wrong.

Minnie said slowly, almost wearily:

"Go away, Rollison. I don't know a thing—now go away."

There were moments when the Toff realized that he could do nothing, short of physical persuasion, which did not occur to him. He knew that he had been watched, that the call had been made to stop Minnie from talking, and there was no doubt that it would prove effective – for a while.

There were other ways of frightening Minnie.

He shrugged, as if he did not know what had altered her manner, and he was almost fatherly as he reached the door.

"You'll regret it, Minnie, but you've still time to repent. Phone me, or send for me. And Minnie—Sidey died painfully."

He was outside almost before she realized it, and went downstairs very thoughtfully. He remained thoughtful when he saw and recognized Benson lounging at a corner, with three other men. Nearby there was a telephone kiosk, and not unnaturally it occurred to him that the call had been made from there. He walked smartly towards the Lambeth Bridge Road. It was easy enough to shake off Benson, who had followed him – and in three minutes the Toff was entering a small house where he was well known.

Throughout London there were countless families who owed much to the Toff. There were wives and children of men in prison who needed help, and he helped them willingly, and even set their men up in reasonable jobs when they came out. There were people – some of the police included – who believed that Rollison did more good than the Prisoners' Aid Society, although he scoffed at the suggestion when he heard it. Yet in his way he was proud of his connection with them – and in truth they helped him often.

The large, blowsy but genial-faced woman who opened the door to him lifted her arms in obvious delight, and ushered him into a small kitchen, where the fire was smoking and the atmosphere thick. She was pleased and thrilled to see the Toff, and said so – and immediately put a kettle on to make some tea.

"Always noo yer'd look us up again, Mr. R. 'Iggins is still workin' on the straight, thanks to you. I reckon I gotta lot to thank you for. You will stay fer a cuppa cha, woncha?"

"When I've changed," said the Toff. "You've some clothes of 'Iggins I can wear?"

"You can ..." Mrs. Higgins stared, and then she nodded, tight-lipped, even a little disapproving. But she found Higgins's clothes, and they fitted the Toff reasonably well. He supplied his own caps, which he had in a manuscript pocket in his coat – three different caps, for different reasons.

The tea was made when he had changed.

Mrs. Higgins, like most of her kind, asked no questions and wanted no information. But as he drank the thick, black brew she had made, she voiced the hope that he was not going to run his head into a noose.

"The noose is for someone else," said the Toff with a smile. "Don't worry about me, Ma. I'll bring the clothes back or send them in a day or two. All right?"

"Bless me 'eart, yer don't 'ave to worry abaht them, Mister. Ar. Take 'em 'an welcome."

"They'll come back," said the Toff; "we can't have Higgins running about naked."

This made her ample bosom shake with hearty laughter, and while it was shaking the Toff lifted a hand in farewell, and went out. It was pleasant to be in the cool, clean air of the street again, but he had spent more time there than he wanted, and he hurried again towards Minnie's flat.

It was possible that she had gone out before him.

He could not be sure, but when he glanced up the road he thought he saw Benson, still lounging and talking to two idlers, cigarettes dangling from their lips.

Rollison had touched up his face, using coal-dust, and he looked very unlike the Toff as he passed the end of the street. Then he waited at a corner where he could see Minnie's flat, spending some of the time wishing that he had taken that telephone call, yet wondering whether it would have made much difference.

Minnie had.

She had been well aware that her husband was working with Benson, and had been informed by a message that had been delivered promptly – although unknown to the police – that if she kept quiet about that association, she would be richer by five hundred pounds.

Five hundred pounds in the hand was worth a lot more to Minnie than a murderer on the trap, and she had accepted the bribe, which had been delivered to her in the same way as the offer. In point of fact, through the charwoman who called ever morning for the 'heavy work' at the flat. Benson knew a thing or two about getting past the police.

He and others were anxious, she had known, to talk to her, but until that morning the detective outside had prevented her from going out to see them. In any case, it was too dangerous for him to call on her. That morning she had felt safe until the Toff's visit. After it, she went to a great deal of trouble to make sure she was not being watched by the police or Rollison. As she knew many of the plain-clothes men in the Force, and boasted she could tell one a mile off, she had good reason for feeling that she was safe from them, if not from Rollison.

She did not see the Toff, shabbily dressed in Higgins's clothes, as he lounged at the corner. The Toff was carrying his three caps – a brown, a black, and a brilliant check. By changing them occasionally and altering their angle he contrived to make sure he was not suspected; for, apart from his caps, he looked absolutely nondescript, and the caps 'proved' him to be three separate people.

By a roundabout route Minnie reached the Blue Dog.

The Toff's eyes gleamed, and he would have given a great deal to have gone inside. But he was glad that he had not, for within five minutes Minnie reappeared, this time accompanied by a stranger to the Toff.

He was a short man, broad of shoulder, and with a handsome, if Hebraic, face – the kind of face that would have aroused comment in most places. He was smiling, perhaps too freely. His clothes, the Toff admitted, were well-cut, although the check of his suit was too loud for Rollison's taste, and might be called flashy.

The situation was becoming more complicated as the Toff slouched behind the man and woman, keeping on the other side of the road. He hoped the chase would not last long, and his hope was fulfilled when the couple turned into a coffee-shop near the docks – none other than Sammy's, where Anthea had been – and the Toff slipped in behind them.

He could not see the couple behind the high-backed seats, but Minnie's voice, high-pitched and shrill, told him where they were. He frowned as he slipped into the seat nearest them but out of sight. Why should she meet the man at all, and why should he come to this place with its good reputation? More – why should they order two large Bovrils?

A thin wooden partition separated them from the Toff, and he could hear every word of their conversation. It was not a particularly informative one, and the only thing of interest the Toff learned was that the man's name was Ritzy.

He had found Martin!

And then Minnie lowered her voice, and the Toff only just caught the words.

"When's Mr. Ruddy Benson coming, Ritzy? I don't trust that feller, an' I ain't even likely to."

Ritzy laughed; his voice was pleasant and low-pitched as ever, and as confidential.

"Don't worry about him, Minnie. He'll turn up, and he won't double-cross you. Listen, don't you want salt in that?"

At the moment the words struck the Toff as being as banal as any could be, and but for the mention of Benson's name he would have told himself that his errand was abortive – but for Ritzy. But he was bored by Ritzy and Minnie – who were by then flirting – even if he was puzzled by Ritzy's obvious interest in the woman. He was what even the Toff would have called a different type from Minnie; there was a false note somewhere which he could not find.

Benson was a long time coming. Minnie said so a little louder than before, and in some annoyance, and Ritzy laughed again. That was the last sound for perhaps five minutes, before Ritzy stood up and said he would be seeing her soon.

Minnie did not answer.

The Toff scowled as Ritzy squeezed out of his seat and left the coffee-shop, tempted to follow the man, and yet more directly concerned with Minnie. She would crack, he believed, before long, particularly if the Toff talked to her with Benson there. Another ten minutes passed, and with it the Toff's second cup of coffee. He stood up at last and slouched past the next cubicle.

And he saw Minnie Sidey bent over the table with her head buried in her arms. There was something strange about her stillness, and there was a sharp fear in the Toff's mind as he stepped forward then gripped her wrist.

Her pulse was not beating; Minnie Sidey was as dead as her husband.

Chapter Thirteen

Police at Work

The Toff had reached that possibility when he had first seen Minnie lying there with her head buried in her arms, her body so obviously taut. When he eased her head upwards, and he knew that she had died in pain, and yet had contrived to make no sound.

Or had been prevented by a drug from creating a disturbance?

Whichever way it was, the Toff felt a fierce hatred of the man who had done this thing. The events had moved with a startling suddenness, and he was beginning to understand something of Kohn's faith in himself, beginning to know that he was fighting a man whose methods were ruthless and effective, who struck without the slightest warning and at the least suspected place.

Should he have expected the murder?

In one way, yes; he had even warned Minnie of its possibility, and he wished now that he had not. On the other hand, Sam's café was the last place in the world to expect murder: it had a reputation second to none, and Sam himself, with his moon-face and dark moustache, was as stout a custodian of the law as any policeman.

The Toff's chief regret was that he had stayed with Minnie and let Martin go.

But there was some satisfaction in this direct connection between Martin and the Kohn affair. He was getting a Une on Martin as damning as he had already obtained on Benson, and could testify against them well enough to make reasonably sure that they reached the gallows. If for a moment he wondered whether he should have given the police more information, he decided quickly that so far there was not a sufficiently direct connection between Kohn and Irma.

He had to get one.

He also felt, as he straightened up, that he had to avenge the death of Minnie Sidey. It was odd how it affected him, perhaps because he had seen the fear in her eyes when she had left the telephone. A fear great enough to outweigh that of the Toff. Who could have inflicted it?

The police had to know quickly, and there must be a call put out for Martin – the man had been at large too long. But to call for him over this murder would be playing his cards too soon, and as the Toff went towards the kitchen – where Sam and Gert were eating their dinner – he had decided on his course of action.

He took off his cap, and Sam stared up uncertainly.

"Sam," said the Toff, "a word in your ear."

"Gor' bless my soul!" said Sam, and he pushed his chair back, wiping his hands on the inside of his apron as he had done when he had been introduced to Anthea. "It's Mister A! I thought I reckernized yer, but in that git-up – blimey, you know a thing or two, you do!"

There was a quality of astuteness about Sam, for he had not mentioned Rollison by name. That, of course, was for the benefit of the two draymen who were eating at the cubicle nearest the door. Rollison took a couple of steps up the gangway leading to Minnie, and then said quietly:

"There's trouble, Sam. I'm sorry, but it couldn't be avoided."

Sam stared.

"Trouble 'ere?"

"Right here," said the Toff, "and you'll have to close up. Are you on the telephone?"

"Y-yus, but …"

"Easy does it," said the Toff. "One of your visitors has been throwing poison about, Sam, and this woman's dead."

He did not need to put the news any less abruptly, for with Cockney's *sang-froid* Sam took it all in his stride. He glanced at the girl, clicked his lips, and then nodded: "I'll wait, you phone, Mister R. Gert, let the gennulman come through to the phone."

Gert, as dirty and untidy as when she had served Anthea, made way sullenly. The telephone was fixed to the wall near the sink, the sides of which were spotlessly clean where they might have been expected to be dirty. The girl slipped into the shop itself while the Toff lifted the receiver and called McNab.

McNab was a remarkable officer in so far as he was always in – or nearly always – when the Toff wanted him. His voice was muffled, suggesting that he was having a sandwich in the warmth of his office.

"Mac," said the Toff soberly, "you want some men from C3 Division quickly. Sam's coffee-shop; they'll know the place. Fingerprints, cameras and whatnot – here's your chance for getting on to a job while it's hot."

"Rollison, what …?" began McNab.

There was momentary silence, and then a sound which seemed suspiciously like a choke. McNab, in fact, had swallowed too quickly, but he recovered to go on: "What is it?"

"Minnie Sidey," said the Toff.

"She's dead?"

"Very dead. Poison."

"Be God!" said McNab, which was not like him. "I'll be over myself, Rollison. You stay there."

Rollison promised that he would, and went back to Sam, who was on guard over the body, which had not been seen by the two draymen. Gert was outside, chalking a notice on the Bill of Fare board to say that the shop was closed. Three or four times in the next five minutes footsteps sounded outside, and loud voices demanded admission. Sam went to the door and shooed the callers away, while the Toff picked up the salt-pot on the table where Minnie was lying.

He remembered the incongruity of the remark about salt.

He tasted the "salt" on the edges of the small pourer-holes, grimaced, and removed the stuff with his handkerchief. There was little or no doubt where the poison came from, little question but that when Ritzy had helped her to salt he had sent her to her death.

A pleasant-voiced, smiling man – and a killer, this Ritzy Martin.

The police arrived at last, first from C3 Division with cameras and finger-print equipment, with an Inspector who knew the Toff by sight and was not affable. McNab was along in a remarkably short space of time and the Toff gave his story – saying only that he had recognized the man who had been with Minnie but could not place him.

"You can describe him," said McNab quickly.

"Of course, Mac …"

The Toff described him so well that McNab had a call put through to the Yard, and a summons issued for the detention of the man who answered that description, which was as detailed as the Toff could make it. It had to be, for Sam and Gert, not to mention the draymen, would also give descriptions and any anomalies would quickly be checked up.

"How did you know she was here?" McNab said.

"I was heeding your request," said Rollison amiably. "You've got all the description you need of the man, Mac, and I'll testify when you get him. It would be an idea," he added, lifting the salt-pot carefully, "to test this for prints."

McNab had this done, but there was none on it.

There was evidence enough, however, that poison had been mixed with the salt, and the Toff imagined that it was one of the quick-acting hypnotics. He knew of nothing else which would have done the job so quickly, and with such little fuss. The pot, with everything else on the table, was sent to the Yard for examination, while McNab and the Toff, with two cameramen and a finger-print officer, went to the Sidey's flat.

It was just as Minnie had left it.

On the floor of the bathroom was the towel which she had draped round her when the Toff had called: he knew that it was the same one because of the safety-pin still sticking in it. There was the telephone, and there was a pair of old house-shoes which she had been wearing, one by the door, the other beneath the table. She had been a slattern about the house, proof of which was in the accumulated dirty crockery in the scullery, the unmade bed, the fluff and dust everywhere.

But she had been human and alive – and she was dead.

There was one thing that he had not told McNab, and that was of the visit to the Blue Dog before her meeting with Ritzy that, and, of course, his guess at the man's name. When all was said and done, the nickname 'Ritzy' could apply to someone else, and the fact that he believed it to be Martin was not proof.

His chief anxiety was to prevent that precipitate action.

But he was playing with fire, and he had never been more aware of it as he and McNab went through the flat, discovering very little – and nothing at all which could connect Minnie with the murder of her husband, or with any knowledge of it.

There was an envelope, plain but torn open, lying in one corner of the bedroom. There were, in fact, several envelopes and several letters, all from friends of Minnie's and all meaning nothing to McNab and the Toff. The plain envelope might have been thrown away, for it was empty, but the Toff took it from McNab.

"A stout one, Mac."

"What of it?"

"I've known banks use them, for registration," said the Toff. "I wonder if … Mac, we've found something."

He spoke almost with excitement as he peered at the flap of the envelope. On it were several pencilled figures, some of them partly destroyed when the envelope had been opened. But by diligence and perseverance, they deciphered:

$$250 - 10\text{'s}$$
$$250 - 5\text{'s}$$

"Recognize it?" asked the Toff.

"Aye," said McNab, and then abruptly: "Do you?"

"To me," said Rollison, "it looks like the pencilled notes of a bank cashier. Two-fifty pounds in tens, two-fifty in fives. Tenners and fivers, Mac."

"Aye. I'll have it checked."

"Your discovery, of course," said the Toff.

He said it without bitterness, and he was glad that there was something into which McNab could get his teeth. It was obvious to the Toff that McNab was not having a good time from his superiors, and some results were badly needed in order to restore a prestige which – at the Yard – could be easily damaged.

At least, thought Rollison, McNab could learn of Benson within twenty-four hours, and that would give him a fillip.

Twenty-four hours …

In that time the Toff had to get the proof he wanted against Kohn. It was madness to leave it longer, madness to keep all he knew from the police for more than that time.

Could he get to the end within twenty-four hours?

He could at least hope so, and he left Minnie's flat with McNab, but did not go to Scotland Yard. From a convenient telephone kiosk he telephoned Jolly.

"Come to the Blue Dog," said the Toff, "and look tough. You're to hold a watching brief."

"Very good, sir. In half an hour I will be there."

"Don't make it longer. I'm hungry. Anything to report?"

"Lady Anthea has been on the telephone several times, sir."

"Telephone her and say I'll call within two hours," said Rollison. "Get a move on, Jolly; things aren't going to stay quiet much longer."

"I'm glad to hear it, sir."

There was a good reason for the tone of Jolly's voice, which suggested that he felt things had gone far too badly. Jolly often had ideas which were in line with the Toff's, feeling frustrated when the Toff was not getting ahead as he wanted to, or on top of the world when the Toff knew that it was a matter of hours before the game turned out as he wanted it.

There was no justification for such optimism now, and while the Toff waited in a place of obscurity and within sight of the Blue Dog, he thought of Leopold Kohn.

Kohn was becoming an obsession.

"I think," Rollison mused, "that I'll call and see the gentleman. It should be interesting, and it might make him crack."

That he might not, was his chief worry. There was no sign of Kohn cracking, and, so far, he had countered each of the Toff's moves with one equally astute. He was, in fact, on the attack all the time; he had not been forced on to the defensive as the Toff wanted.

The Toff's expression, while he waited, was bleak.

He was looking at his watch and hoping for Jolly to arrive ahead of time, when a stout man waddled towards the Blue Dog, hesitated for a moment, and then went inside. He had been muffled up in a greatcoat, with a scarf tucked about his chin, a Homburg hat pulled low over his eyes, and with dark-lensed glasses which on their own would have been enough to make the Toff wonder whether he was precisely what he seemed.

He had no idea that it was 'Mr. Brown'.

It was one of those things, as the Toff would have said, which were quite unavoidable. Had he attacked then, had he visited Charlie Wray and found 'Brown' there, the affair would have been over. As it was, he saw Jolly approaching and he sent Jolly – who was also mufflered and capped, and looked the part of an East End labourer to the life – to the Blue Dog, with instructions. After ten minutes Jolly came out, slouching towards the Toff.

"No such man there, sir. All the usual type at the moment."

"Try to remember to drop your aitches," said the Toff, "and keep the place under observation, Jolly. If the mufflered man comes out, follow him."

"Very good, sir."

"Those aitches!" insisted the Toff. "At the moment you sound like a gentleman's gentleman and look like a bookmaker's tout. Was Lady Anthea very insistent?"

"*Very*, sir, but not communicative." Jolly conveyed the impression of being affronted, and the Toff smiled when he recalled Anthea's virtual admission that she considered Jolly out of place as the Toff's man-servant. But he had asked her to give Jolly any message of importance, and he was vaguely puzzled to find that she had not done so.

He decided on the spur of the moment to go to Gresham Terrace as Mr. Higgins, and to send the borrowed clothes back later.

There he had what he later considered his one lucky break. When he first reached his flat, however, he doubted whether it was lucky – he could think of nothing but Anthea.

For Anthea was lying half-in and half-out of the front door of his flat, face downwards, and quite still.

She looked as immobile as Minnie Sidey had been, and in that moment the Toff was terribly afraid.

Chapter Fourteen

Luck for the Toff

He acted quickly.

He bent down, lifted her bodily from the floor, and carried her to a settee, and then he returned to the door and closed it, marvelling that no one else had seen her as she lay there. Her body was warm, and he had seen the slight movement of her lips, proof that she was breathing. He could see nothing else to account for her prostration, but as he closed the door he saw two things.

Across it, on the inside, had been stretched a piece of cord, as on the outside a few nights ago, but now the cord was loose, obviously where Anthea had walked into it: that explained her fall. Near it was a knife.

Not a pleasant-looking knife, it was fastened to the door-jamb with a length of stout coiled spring wire, newly screwed in. He caught his breath as he saw it, for he knew what had happened, and he was appalled. As much because of Anthea's narrow escape as for himself. He saw, as he examined it, that the spring was so fixed that as the door opened to its fullest extent the knife would swing back viciously; and it was at the height of his neck. Had he entered and fallen forward, as he must have done, the knife would have cut through his jugular if not his throat. The thing had missed Anthea, who was shorter. He saw, too, that she had cracked her head against a chair closer to the door than it should have been, and obviously used by the man who had fixed the knife.

Satisfied that she had only been knocked out, but that there was nothing seriously the matter with her, he went cautiously into each of the other rooms. They were empty, but the door leading from the kitchen to the fire-escape was open, and the lock showed evidence of having been forced. The rest was easy.

After Jolly had left someone had been in, fixed the murderous contraption, and escaped quickly. Someone who had known how to work fast, and who had been watching, to make sure that the flat was empty before he started operations. Kohn – on the attack. And Anthea perilously close to death. Had he returned later, after changing at Mrs. Higgins, anything might have happened, for he expected an early visit from Kohn's men. They would want to get the flat door closed and thus postpone the discovery of the crime. He suspected, too, that he had been seen entering, and in all likelihood his man would be up soon.

He hesitated, and then looked through the front door which he opened only a few inches. No one was outside, but there were footsteps on the stairs. He put his hand to his pocket, and the gun which he always carried when he was busy – and as his fingers touched the cold steel he heard Anthea's: *"Rolly!"*

The footsteps stopped, but only for a fraction of a second. Whoever was there turned, and ran down, and the Toff went out, moving as fast as any man could. But he was too late to see more than a man whom he imagined to be Benson climbing on to a motor-cycle parked outside.

Pursuit was quite useless.

A shot fired then would only cause trouble and more encounters with the police, and would do little good. The Toff said many things under his breath before he went back upstairs, to find Anthea on her feet, but holding onto a table. Her right foot was only just touching the carpet.

She looked dishevelled, with her fair hair unruly and her dress hitched up at the waist, while her lips were parted and there was a queer, strained expression in her eyes. It eased as she saw the Toff, although she looked puzzled. Nothing, he decided, would ever prevent Anthea from looking lovely.

"Well, my pet." There was a touch of irony in his voice, for he wondered why she was here, even wished that she had not come. "You've disobeyed doctor's orders – so what?"

"Please, Rolly, don't be difficult. What—what are you dressed like that for?"

"I've been out to lunch. Latest wear for the man-about-town! And that reminds me, it's tea-time. Or would you like something stronger?"

"No, thanks, but a cup of tea sounds divine. I ... Rolly, what on earth happened? I came in, and tripped over something, and" – she lifted her hands in bewilderment – "I remember falling, but after that it's blank."

"You were knocked out," said Rollison easily. He stepped to her side, lifted her unprotestingly, and sat her on the settee where she could keep her legs up. "You were also very lucky. How did you open the door?"

"It was ajar."

"Hmm. Careless work on someone's part."

"Who—who was it?" She seemed intent on an answer, but before he spoke she went on a little breathlessly: "I feel an awful fool, Rolly. Before I was knocked out I—I thought I was going to die. I heard a whanging sound. I thought it was a bullet. It's not—not a nice feeling."

"You're right in one," said Rollison, stepping through to the kitchen after locking and bolting the front door. "It's a long way from nice, but it wasn't a bullet, our friends can think up something far more original than that. What time did you get here?" This from the kitchen, where he had put a kettle on and was looking for a tea-pot.

"Just about a quarter to three, I suppose."

"And Jolly reached me at twenty past two," said the Toff thoughtfully. "This job was arranged soon after he left, and my Mr. Kohn goes up even further in my estimation. A cleverer man than I thought, Anthea, and a very worthy partner for Irma."

Anthea brushed back her hair. She was sitting upright, and the Toff could see the strained expression in her blue eyes.

"Rolly, why don't you tell the police everything? It's far too dangerous as it is. Anything might happen to you, and to others. Is—is it fair to them?" Anthea finished sharply. She was looking very intense, very serious.

Rollison put three teaspoonsful of tea into the pot, while the electric kettle began to sing.

"No," he said, "and yes, Anthea. It's a queer business as you've seen before, and I'm a queer fellow, as you've said before. Rightly or wrongly, I've a system, or more correctly a theory, and that theory depends on keeping my machinations from the police until the last moment, *unless* I'm convinced that any other course would be fatal. At the moment I'm not convinced of that, and so I'm keeping certain things to myself. Someone else may die," he said very slowly, lifting the kettle and brewing the tea, yet concentrating on what he was saying, "but it can't be helped, Anthea. If—I say if—the police get on to Irma and her boyfriend, the most likely result is a triple-murder of people who might give conclusive evidence against them."

"But surely the police can arrest this woman and the man?"

"On what grounds?" The Toff loaded a tray and carried it into the drawing-room, setting it on a chair while he brought the coffee table to her side.

"Well, on the evidence you can give."

"The legal understanding of the word 'evidence' and mine don't concur," said Rollison, and she knew that he was being wholly serious, even sensed that she was hearing something of his deeper motives, the real reason for his interest in crime particularly in that sprawling part of the Metropolis called the East End. "Anthea, if I tell McNab about Irma and the boyfriend, they will be interviewed – but there just isn't enough legal evidence to detain them. The lesser fry of the outfit, yes. But the lesser fry will be under cover all the time, and Irma and her friend will get to them before the police. It's not nice, my dear. It's never pleasant to think that if you had acted differently you might have saved lives. But better for those lives to go, the lives of the people who have died in this affair, than that Kohn and Irma should remain free. What they're doing now they've done a dozen times before, and will again. Not necessarily here, but there are other places in the world than London, where fools can be mulcted of their money, and the Irma type can live in a luxury taken from the dead." He paused, and his eyes were smiling a little, but sombrely he looked at her as he started to pour out tea. "Have I made myself clear?"

"Ye-es. I—mind that tea, idiot!" A cup was brimful, and her warning stopped it running over. Rollison chuckled, and it was hard to believe that he had been talking so seriously a few seconds before.

Anthea laughed, a little helplessly, for there was so much about the Toff which was likeable, and so much incomprehensible. The tea was medium strong, and good. She sipped it as she eyed him, while he followed her example, breaking off only to light a cigarette. The knife and the tension spring might never have been in the room.

"And now, my sweet," said the Toff lightly, "what brought you here?"

Anthea started – and in starting her cup tipped over. Rollison shot a hand out and averted a major catastrophe, but several drops had fallen on her skirt. She ignored it, brushing away Rollison's proffered handkerchief.

"I'd forgotten! Rolly, I'm an awful fool. I had to see you, to talk to you, and I didn't think I could make Jolly understand."

"We'll omit that angle. What is it?"

"It's about Wrightson's fiancée—Phyllis Bailey."

The Toff's eyes narrowed.

"What about her?"

"One of the people I phoned yesterday was a friend of hers. You – you know she's supposed to have eloped?"

"*Supposed?*" said the Toff, and his voice sharpened. "She has eloped—I hope," he added very softly.

"This friend was talking to her only a couple of days ago, and Phyllis—it's easier to call her Phyllis—seemed worried. She was quite definite on one point—that she would not allow a break between Wrightson and his uncle."

"Wouldn't she, indeed?"

"She was absolutely positive," said Anthea quietly. "Or so I was told. And this friend suggests that the last thing Phyllis would do would be to elope. They share a study together, or something like that, and she seems quite sure Phyllis would have said something about it."

"Elopements," said the Toff very slowly, "are funny things. Wrightson certainly looked in the mood to do anything on impulse. Is that all?"

"Nearly all. According to the papers, Rolly, they eloped some time in the early evening. Phyllis was playing bridge with some friends at Hampstead until past ten. She left to go to her home in Chelsea, and if she did elope she must have met Wrightson on the way, because she didn't go home, or stay with her friend that night."

The Toff was looking very bleak, and his right fore-finger was rubbing along the side of his nose, a sure sign that he was worried.

"I—see. Anthea, I have been all kinds of a damned fool in the past, but never so badly as this time. I took that story for gospel, but it could as easily be a fake. What made you worry about it?"

"Well, you told me enough for me to gather that there might be a connection with this Irma woman."

"Ye-es." Rollison stood up, his tea forgotten. "I'm going to change, Anthea. You can reach the telephone—call a friend to come to collect you. I don't want to leave you here alone."

"Where are you going?"

"To Renway's house, and other places."

He washed and changed quickly, while Anthea used the new telephone that had been fitted only that morning, and arranged for a friend to come by car to take her away. She urged the friend to hurry, and the Toff had been ready only two minutes when the car arrived. Before entering the drawing-room again, he had fitted a small knife to the calf of his leg, using a leather sheath which clipped through his suspender, and he carried a gun in a shoulder holster as well as one in his pocket.

He said little as he helped Anthea downstairs.

She sensed that he was feeling as grim as he looked; there was something about his manner which was almost frightening. She wondered whether she had done good or harm by coming, and then forgot that when she realized how nearly she had died.

She wondered, later, whether the Toff was cursing her for interfering.

Nothing could have been further from the truth, for the Toff was blessing her and cursing himself. The elopement could have been a fake, and he, like a purblind idiot, had taken it at its face value.

Renway was out, but with a little encouragement, the footman proved talkative. Yes, Mr. Wrightson had been in the whole of the morning and afternoon, before he had gone off. It was a surprising thing, for he had seemed quite normal -except that he seemed worried: but then, it was well known that he was not on the best terms with his uncle. What time did he leave? About six-thirty, not long before dinner.

The Toff thanked him, and tipped him again, and then went into the question of Phyllis Bailey's bridge-party. Not until then did he discover for sure that she had left on the day before Wrightson – and the 'elopement' positively shouted suspicion.

The Toff decided that another interview with Leopold Kohn was essential.

The Toff liked to think that one of his most effective weapons was that of surprise, but he was beginning to wonder whether surprise would be effective against Kohn. He was more apprehensive about that gentleman than he had been about anyone for a long time. The assumption that Wrightson and his fiancée had been kidnapped seemed, now, to be the obvious one.

If it was a fact, the question was – why?

Could young Wrightson be needed for the completion of Kohn's campaign?

The mystery of it, and the utter lack of direct evidence to indicate what was the motive of the crimes, also presented its worrying aspect. All in all, the Toff was prepared to admit that he was coming off worse than he had in any previous case. He went straight up to the flat in Arch Mansions, and examined the lock of the front door.

It was a cursory inspection, for he knew that it was a Yale, while he had seen before that it had been reinforced to make a burglarious entry difficult if not impossible. There was a fire-escape, and he could have got through that way – but not, he decided, if Kohn was on the premises.

He rang the bell.

There was no answer, and he rang again. Satisfied that Kohn was out, he tried the next-door flat; there was no response from Irma, and into the Toff's eyes there sprang a gleam more of adventure than of hope.

The fire-escape at Arch Mansions was in full view of anyone who happened to be in the courtyard below, and of the tenants of nearby flats. By night that would not have been important, but Rollison could not wait until after dark. He had to take a chance, and the key to the effort was speed. The longer he waited outside, trying to force a lock or window, the more risk of being seen.

He kept on his glove when he reached Kohn's flat and, without ado, cracked his fist through a pane of glass in the door. The sharp tinkling noise seemed louder to him than it really was, but he did not wait to find whether anyone's attention had been aroused. He slipped his arm through the hole, found the catch, and slid it back. Not until the door was open, and he had gone through, did he look out – and he saw no one, heard nothing which suggested that he had raised an alarm.

He closed the door, and slipped into the main rooms.

The flat was empty, and Rollison wasted no time admiring the furniture. He did not know whether he had five minutes or fifty in which to work, and the more he did in the first five the better his chances would be. But even as he started turning out the drawers of the desk in the study, he felt that there was little likelihood of a discovery of importance. There had been no burglar alarm at the back door, which suggested that Kohn kept nothing here that mattered; obviously Irma would have warned him of a likely visit from the Toff, and if there had been papers of importance here they would have been secured under lock and key, and the flat protected by an alarm.

As far as he could find, there were no papers.

What was more puzzling, the safe – as fitted in all the flats, and just behind Kohn's desk – contained nothing but a few bundles of notes of small denominations, mostly ten shilling and one pound. Twenty-five five-pound notes reminded him of the pencilled letters on the plain envelope found at Minnie Sidey's flat, but that did not help. There were no tens.

He went through the two bedrooms and the dining-room and the lounge when he had finished with the study – and he found nothing at all which would help him. There were some indications of Kohn's exotic taste in literature, while he discovered a photograph album which was not pleasant. All it suggested was what the Toff already knew – Leopold Kohn was an unlikeable human being.

Half an hour passed quickly.

It was not the first time that Rollison had searched a flat, and when he had finished he was sure that there was nothing he had overlooked, always allowing for the possibility of hidden compartments in the desk, or even in the walls. He tapped the latter, but only cursorily. To have made a thorough investigation of them would have taken him a day; he did not think there was much chance that he would strike a hiding-place by accident.

There was nothing incriminating there.

He shrugged, and went into the bathroom to wash his hands. That done, he entered the study again, selected a cigarette from the box on Kohn's desk, and sat back in Kohn's swivel chair. It was comfortable, and the Toff had plenty to think about. But while he thought, and while he waited, he was on the *qui vive*, listening for the first sound of approach.

It came just after five o'clock.

Footsteps outside, and then a key in the lock. The murmur of voices, Irma's coming through the opening door before Kohn's.

Kohn answered: "You're much too nervous, Irma; you must try to take a firmer hold on yourself. Everything is going very satisfactorily very satisfactorily indeed."

The Toff moved from the desk.

He had not smoked since the first cigarette and he hoped there was enough smoke in the room to be noticed. He slipped into a small single bedroom, half-closing the door, while Kohn and Irma entered the study.

Irma said: "I've told you before Leo. The fact that he's doing nothing doesn't mean that he's not satisfied with the situation. And he might be doing a lot you don't expect."

Kohn laughed, not pleasantly.

"He visited the Sidey woman this morning, and we knew it the moment he entered by the front door. We put her away under his nose—and then he had luck again, and escaped at his flat. But he's lucky to be alive, and he's no fool—he'll realise his luck. I tell you we've clipped his claws, Irma, and I don't want any more talk about him."

Irma said, very ominously: "What you want and what you'll get are different things, and it's time you understood it. Under-estimating Rollison is suicide."

Kohn was silent for a moment, and when he went on his voice was bland: "My dear Irma, there isn't the slightest need for you to get worked up like this. I'll look after Rollison, and before we're through you will be able to take off the black. Now everything else is set."

"Renway is …"

"We needn't go into it again," said Kohn. "I've some figures to work out, Irma, and I'm going to be busy. I can leave Renway to you. I'm not a bit worried on that score. You'll forgive me if I don't see you to the door?"

The Toff's lips were curving, for it was good to hear Irma talked to in this way – although whether it would eventually prove good for Kohn was a different matter. It was the first intimation he had had that there was any trouble in the Irma-Leo friendship, and had it been earlier in the affair it might have been useful.

At the moment it was more obstructive than anything else.

He had hoped there would be talk that would prove serviceable, but Kohn was bent on working, and there was no object in the Toff keeping under cover any longer. He moved quietly, pushing the door open, and he saw Irma staring at Kohn with an expression in her eyes which suggested she was a long way from pleased.

"Be very careful," she said. "You can go too far."

"Now, Irma, be sensible …"

"Excellent advice, if I may say so," murmured the Toff.

He stood against the door, although one moment ago it had seemed that there was no one there. In his hand was an automatic, and from his lips dangled an unlighted cigarette. In the moment of startled silence which followed he struck a match, and the first streamer of smoke left his lips. He regarded them through it. Kohn, with his rather sharp, ascetic face, the dark eyes which could be so malevolent, the slightly over-long hair, brushed in a style that might have been expected in a musician, the touches of grey, which lent him such a bogus dignity, at the temples; Irma, in black, with white frills at wrists and neck. Undoubtedly she looked beautiful.

And startled out of her life.

For a moment, too, Kohn had been put off his balance, but he recovered quickly, and the only sign of feeling was shown in the tightening of his lips. The Toff smiled as if he were delighted to see them.

"Tongue-tied?" he asked.

"What are you doing here?" demanded Kohn.

"A very ordinary question," said the Toff amiably. "I look for some originality from you, Leo, and I'm disappointed to find you so banal. Ritzy's rather banal, too."

Kohn said coldly: "I don't know what you're talking about."

"No?" asked the Toff, arching his brows. "I'm surprised, really I am. I thought you and Ritzy were as close as that, and the stuff he put in the salt surely came from you. Where do you keep supplies, Leo? I haven't looked in the bathroom yet, but I doubt if I'll find them there."

Kohn moved back to his desk, and sat down very slowly.

Irma put one hand to her waist, and ordered: "Rollison, get out of here."

"In due course," said the Toff. "It was a delight to hear you, Irma. How could I guess that you had so high an opinion of me? Earned by dint of much struggle, I may say, but all effort is worth while when it succeeds. I have been working in many ways that our Leo doesn't realise. He makes so many mistakes but he doesn't recognise them."

"Bluff won't work," said Kohn.

"An almost pathetic inability to express yourself effectively," said the Toff, and he sounded regretful. "Of course one can't have everything. Control of gentlemen like Benson and Sidey -poor Sidey, and poor Minnie—of Wray and Ritzy, is bound to have its effect in the long urn."

Irma relaxed, and sat down, crossing her knees and staring insolently at the Toff.

"Have you finished?"

"Nearly. What a pity you and Leo didn't have a shouting match when you were about it. I would," said the Toff earnestly, "have refereed with strict impartiality. However, there it is. Where's Jim Wrightson?"

Kohn stiffened.

Irma leaned forward, tense again.

"And his fiancée?" went on the Toff. The lightness and the raillery had gone from his voice, he looked and sounded dangerous. "I don't mind Sidey being murdered, and I wasn't as sorry for Minnie as I might have been, but when it comes to a decent couple like that the line is drawn. Is that clear?"

Kohn's lips were dry.

"You're talking nonsense!"

"You think so? We'll see in a few hours, Kohn. I've collected—as they say in the best circles—all the evidence, and I'm going to use it in the very near future. I'm holding my hand because of Wrightson and the girl, but I'll take a chance with their safety very soon. You'd better release them. And," he added, taking the cigarette from his lips and tossing it towards the fireplace, "you will be wise to act quickly."

He stepped to the front door – and one moment he seemed to be in the room, the next he was outside and the door closed behind him.

He guessed what was happening in the room he had left, for he knew both Irma and Kohn were startled beyond words. He was right in his guess, even to the tense silence which lasted for fully thirty seconds.

Irma broke it.

"Well?" Her voice was hoarse. "Do you believe me now?"

"He was guessing!" snapped Kohn.

"Guessing about Wrightson and the girl? Don't be a fool; he knows we've got them."

"And what the hell do you expect me to do? Go and let them out? Or send a letter of apology to Rollison? If he knew anything worth knowing he would have acted by now, and I'm not worried by any blasted bluff! *I'll* look after Rollison."

"You've tried often enough."

Kohn drew a sharp breath, and for a moment it looked as if he would strike her. But he stopped himself, and swung round to his chair, as Irma swept past him.

The Toff walked blithely, and more happily than for some days, back to Gresham Terrace. With Kohn and Irma at the quarrelling stage his own position was much stronger. And Kohn's attitude had been virtual proof of the fact that the other couple had been kidnapped.

"The good and the bad together," mused the Toff as he let himself into his flat. "I—hello, Jolly, any luck?"

Jolly inclined his head gravely.

"A little, sir, I think." He lit a match for the Toff's cigarette. "According to instructions I followed the man in the muffler. He went to the Turkish Baths in Aldgate, sir, and came out after fifteen minutes. At least," said Jolly apologetically, "I think it was the same men, sir. I believe you would know him better as Leopold Kohn."

Chapter Fifteen

The Toff Attacks

Rollison stepped to the cocktail cabinet and helped himself to a whisky and soda. He took a stiff peg, and put the glass down slowly.

"Well, well," he said, "we're seeing and hearing things. If we'd moved at the Blue Dog we would have had Kohn with Benson, probably Martin, and Charlie Wray. A mistake."

"An unavoidable one, sir, if I may say so."

"There isn't such a thing as an unavoidable mistake," said the Toff sadly. "There have been far too many easily avoidable ones in this business already. Too many late nights, too many *affaires*, too much ..."

"I think you are doing an injustice to Kohn, sir," said Jolly. "He has proved far more effective than was anticipated. And if I dare venture a suggestion ..."

"Go on."

"His motto has been 'attack, always attack'".

"Well?"

"In this, he has taken a leaf out of your own book," said Jolly gently. The Toff laughed, but without humour, as he took out another cigarette; the first he had stubbed out absently. Jolly stepped forward with another match.

"Attack, is it, Jolly? You couldn't suggest in what quarter, could you?"

"An army is as strong as its weakest front, sir."

"Aren't you getting mixed up with a chain and its links? Benson, of course."

"Of course, sir," said Jolly.

"And what does your mind tell you about my relationship with the police, Jolly?"

"The usual method of approach, sir, would seem the best on this occasion. Presenting the police with the case on a plate, sir. Kohn is slippery, and he will have guarded against all likely emergencies. Only the unexpected will catch him sir, and you are the only one likely to find a means of getting past his defence." Jolly was talking almost colloquially for him, and he appeared to be in considerable earnest. "If I dare say so, sir, you have waited too long already. Waiting is quite satisfactory in some cases, when you know what is coming and where to expect it. In this one, the complete mystery which surrounds the activities of Kohn and the woman Cardew make it imperative for you to weigh in, sir, with all you've got. I hope I have made myself clear, sir."

"Abundantly so," murmured the Toff dryly.

"I trust," went on Jolly with some anxiety, "that I have not caused offence, sir. I am a little perturbed by the possibilities as I see them, and …"

The Toff put a hand against Jolly's cheek and pushed his face gently aside.

"You're worth a fortune, Jolly, at least I acknowledge it. However, I rather think I see the glimmering of a hunch."

"Excellent, sir. There has been a shortage of them in this affair, if I may say so."

"Jolly, I will take a bet with you."

"Yes, sir? On what terms?"

"Evens. That Kohn isn't half as clever as we've been led to believe."

"I would even give you odds, sir."

"Evens, I said, in half-crowns." The Toff had started for his bedroom, and he was changing rapidly into dinner clothes, for he considered them more useful for the evening's amusement'. He was on the alert, now, there was a sparkle in his eyes, an expression on

his face that told Jolly that at last something had clicked, the thing
for which the Toff had been waiting for. "In half-crowns," repeated
the Toff, and straggled into his trousers before Jolly could come
forward. "Yes, Jolly, it's all been so involved, far more than we've
realised. It took Lady Anthea to show it to me."

"Indeed, sir?"

"Indeed, yes. Wrightson and his lady have not eloped; they have
been kidnapped."

Jolly looked startled; and perhaps for the first time in his life he let
out an expletive, surprising to them both, mild though it was. The
Toff stared at him for a moment, then laughed softly.

"So you see it, too, do you?"

"I think so, sir."

"Right. You're to be a roughneck again for the night, Jolly, and you
will keep me in sight as well as you can. Benson's the first man to
attack, and after that we go where the spriit moves us, and where the
evidence appears to lead. And listen, Jolly."

"Sir?"

"Wrightson and that girl are in considerable danger."

"I can see that, sir."

"We don't want them to die."

"Certainly not, sir."

"Well, it's up to us," said the Toff, and as he finished tying his bow
tie he went on evenly: "You're sure about the mufflered man being
Kohn?"

"Perfectly sure, sir."

"Excellent," said the Toff. "Excellent work, Jolly. We aren't going
to lower our colours after all."

Jolly agreed that it now appeared unlikely, and they left the flat
within three minutes. They proved to their satisfaction that the flat
was no longer being watched, which suggested that Kohn did not
consider any immediate action from the Toff likely. The Toff went
by taxi to Aldgate Pump, with Jolly in a following cab, and five
minutes afterwards was in the tiny front parlour of a house opposite
the Blue Dog. He could see the pub, and all its three entrances,
clearly.

Throughout the East End there were places like that, which the Toff could use temporarily, either for money or because of what he had done to help the tenants in the past. His name was a watchword throughout that part of London, and many folk said that he was more loved than hated.

Jolly was not far away.

Less than twenty minutes after the Toff had taken up his position Benson arrived at the Blue Dog. He stayed only for 'five minutes, and when he came out the Toff slipped through the open door of the house in which he was hiding, making no sound in his rubber-soled shoes as he followed the man who had killed Sidey.

Benson was passing the end of a cul-de-sac when the Toff's voice came to him: "Benson!"

Benson stopped in his tracks.

"Turn right, Benson," said the Toff.

Benson obeyed. To the right was a narrow turning without a glim of light, the cul-de-sac, which the Toff knew well. The darkness was profound, and Benson felt fear surging within him. But his mind was working quickly, and on the heels of fear came hope. It was dark, and even the Toff could not see what he was doing.

Benson slid his right hand into his pocket and his fingers clutched the cold steel of a gun. He felt a return of confidence, and although now he could hear the soft footsteps of the Toff behind him, he did not feel so much afraid. This was the first time Rollison had tackled him alone.

Benson's lips twisted in a grin of sheer sadism, and he swung round on his heel.

His revolver snapped out. Two stabs of flame – and two bullets hit into a brick wall with lightning impact. In the momentary glare of the shots Benson could see nothing of the Toff, who should have been dead. Fear came again, more shattering this time, because he could have sworn the Toff to be within a couple of yards of him. He stared at nothing, and he shivered.

"I've killed men," said the Toff very gently from behind him, "for much less than that, Benson. Drop your gun."

Benson half-turned, knowing now that the Toff had slipped past him without a sound two or three seconds before the shooting. It was an example of the claims that he could be in two or three places at once, and that he moved faster and more silently than any man living.

Benson hesitated for a fraction of a second, and as he did so the Toff clipped him sharply on the side of the head.

"Move, I said."

Benson moved, and his gun clattered down. The Toff laughed softly through the darkness, yet did not sound amused.

"Scared, little man? Nothing like as much as you will be, Benson. I suppose you aren't short of one hob-nailed boot?"

The words came so unexpectedly, and the darkness lent them so ominous a note, that Benson felt every implication. The pair that had been taken when he had killed Sidey – and the Toff knew where they were!

His face was grey as he cowered back against the wall.

"I don't know nothin'! I don't know wot you mean!"

"Then you've a poor memory," said the Toff, "and you're going to learn a lot before I'm finished with you. You made a corpse of Sidey, Benson, and there's a law that demands a life for a life."

It was a threat, but there were no histrionics. The words came so calmly that their frightening effect was multiplied a hundred times.

"I didn't!" Benson half screamed.

"Keep your voice low," snapped the Toff, and his voice was harsh as he poked a gun in Benson's ribs. Then it dropped to a note that could almost be called a caress, and was the more frightening. "You killed Sidey, Benson, and/saw you. Yes, in spite of the fog. And I took your boots as a souvenir. The police would like them, Benson."

Benson was now shivering as with cold. He felt more afraid than he had ever been in his life, and he seemed to see death yawning in front of him. He seemed to see the face of Kohn, whom he knew as 'Mr. Brown', Irma Cardew, Ritzy, and, above all, Minnie and Alf Sidey. Sidey ..."

He groaned.

"I've heard men moan like that when they've been walking to the long drop," said the Toff. "But your way out won't be so quick, Benson. Before you go, you're going to talk. Why did you kill Sidey?"

Benson's mouth was working and his eyes were feverish.

"I didn't! I swear …"

The Toff struck him. It was a powerful blow, and it took him on the side of the jaw and sent him staggering. He hit the cobbles, but the Toff pulled him up by his coat collar, and then hit him again.

"A taste," he said evenly, "of what will happen to you if you don't come across. I saw you kill Sidey, and I want to know why."

"I—I had to," gasped Benson.

He could not see the gleam that came into the Toff's eyes after that part-admission. The Toff knew that the man was scared for his life, and was going to come across well. The question was – how much did he know?

"The Cardew woman's in this?" Rollison's tone made the words into a question.

Benson's mouth stayed open for a fraction of a second, and then he muttered:

"Y—yes."

"It's as well you admitted it. Now listen, Benson. You've half a chance, a bare half-chance, of saving your neck, if you answer questions. Where do you get your orders from?"

"The Blue Dog." Benson was trembling.

"Where else?"

"There ain't nowheres else, I swear …"

"Keep to the point. You get orders from Charlie Wray, and others I don't know. Who are the others?"

"There ain't …" began Benson.

"You know," said the Toff in his gentlest voice, "I'm sorry to have to do this, Benson, but you've asked for it."

He struck the man again. It gave him no satisfaction, for Benson was incapable of putting up a fight; it was simply the need for forcing information, and it had to be done without thinking of niceties. In three minutes Benson was a helpless hulk of a man, and the Toff was holding him to his feet by his coat lapels.

"Who else?"

"There's—Ritzy," gasped Benson.

"And who's Ritzy?"

"I—I don't know. For Gawd's sake, believe me, mister. I don't know his uvver name! 'E lives at 'Ighgate …"

"What part of Highgate?" asked the Toff, and his grip eased a Utile.

"Abbot Road, Number 28. I—I sees the Boss there."

"You do, do you?" said the Toff, satisfied that he would have no more trouble from Benson now. "Who is the Boss?"

"'E calls hisself Brown. I don't know …"

"I should call you," said the Toff almost amiably, "the most unobservant man of my acquaintance, Benson, but you can stop talking now. We're going for a little journey—no, not to the station yet, but I'm not promising anything. Get going."

While in his mind was thought of 'Brown' and 28, Abbot Road.

The Toff took Benson to the small house nearby, where he knew the man would be safe until he was wanted again. Benson was silent most of the way, although he came across with the information that 'Mr. Brown' wore smoked glasses and was usually well muffled up.

This was the evidence to connect Kohn with the murder of Sidey, the evidence which the Toff had been wanting so badly.

Jolly consulted him after Benson was safely lodged.

"We're doing well," said the Toff, "and certainly as well as can be expected. I wasn't followed?"

"No, sir."

"No sign of anyone else at the Blue Dog?"

"No one of interest, sir. Wray is behind the bar."

"Stay and watch the place," said Rollison, "and follow Wray or Martin, or better still our muffled man if he comes along."

"Very good, sir." Jolly did not raise objections, and the Toff thought over his own handling of Benson. Not nice, and certainly not the type of persuasion that McNab would have approved. But then, McNab would never have obtained that vital information. Benson was scared of the law, but he would have kept a tight mouth, relying on 'Mr. Brown' to pay for his defence and provide him with an alibi. And Brown would have done so, of course, for his own sake.

The Toff was smiling.

He had the Frazer-Nash near Aldgate Pump, and very soon he hoped to be interviewing Ritzy at Highgate. Ritzy would have a bigger shock than Benson, but it was possible that he would also have a greater power of resistance. The Toff did not mind that. There were many degrees in his methods of persuasion, and he had by no means reached the limit of them.

After reaching the Frazer-Nash he found a telephone kiosk and spoke to a lesser official at Scotland Yard, leaving a message for McNab. That would serve two purposes and please the Scotsman.

He located Abbott Road without trouble.

He made no attempt to hide himself, but rang the bell with complete assurance, after parking his car a hundred yards along the street. His summons was answered promptly, for some twenty seconds later, after the ringing had echoed through the house, he found himself looking into the absurdly handsome face of the man called Ritzy.

Ritzy was smiling; he was always smiling, and just then his voice was more pleasant than ever, for he did not recognise the Toff.

"Good evening, sir. What can I do for you?"

The Toff hesitated for a fraction of a second, and then he smiled genially enough to compete with Ritzy. He first put his foot against the door, and then said: "I've come for the salt, Mr. Martin."

He had never seen such a transformation in his life.

One moment Ritzy's face was set in that wide smile; the next it was twisted in an expression of positive alarm. His face turned pale as he stared at the Toff.

"Tongue-tied?" murmured Rollison. "A little chat will help you and I, Ritzy. Step back."

Ritzy obeyed, still dumbstruck, persuaded by the gun in the Toff's hand, as the door closed gently behind him.

"You seem off colour," he said gently. "Lead me to the parlour, son, where we can talk."

JOHN CREASEY

Not until then did Ritzy speak. He made a big effort, and even found a vestige of his smile.

"I—I don't quite know …"

"So few do," said the Toff, who did not propose to allow his initial advantage to slip away. "I can give you your victim's name, Ritzy, I can tell you where you met her, where you took her, and how you killed her. The game's up, you see. But" – the Toff dropped his voice, and spoke almost as if he was afraid that someone would be listening – "I'm not a policeman. Does that suggest anything to you?"

Obviously, it did.

Ritzy's colour did not return, but he forced a sickly grin and turned towards a room leading from the left of the passage and pushed the door open. The Toff made no comment as the man took a decanter from the sideboard and poured himself out a stiff whisky. He did not even reproach him for forgetting his visitor.

"I—I don't know what to say," said Ritzy, and the Toff told himself that this fellow was not going to be much of a handful, that he would be as easy as Benson.

"You can say just enough to answer my questions," said the Toff. "Benson's squealed. Did you know that?"

"Benson! The ruddy …"

"No hard names," implored the Toff. "He's squealed, and you're going to do the same. Don't forget, Martin, what a word from me to the police could do."

He did not need to finish. Ritzy's capitulation proved to be as complete as Benson's, and the Toff gave an inward sigh of relief.

"Go—go on," muttered Ritzy.

"First," said the Toff, "Irma Cardew and Leo Kohn are backing this thing. Renway's in it, as the mug. But just what's the game, Ritzy?"

"I—I don't know …"

"The same old parrot cry," murmured the Toff. "I don't want to have to hurt you, but …"

"I don't know." Ritzy almost squealed. "I worked for Renway, and I've given Kohn information, but I don't know why!"

The Toff's eyes were hard.

"You worked for Kohn as a spy, did you? And what information have you given him?"

He made a mental note as he spoke of the fact that Ritzy knew Kohn's real name – or what passed at the Marble Arch flats for his real name – and saw yet another link in the chain of evidence.

"Figures and—and cheques," Martin muttered.

Ritzy's face was working, as though he realised that if Kohn discovered he had talked his life was worth nothing, but the Toff continued to pound him with relentless questions.

"Cheques. Renway's account books. Recent ones?"

"Ye-es. I ..."

"You what?"

"I—I worked for Renway until a couple of months ago, clearing up his accounts. He was retiring ..."

"I know," said the Toff. "Now answer promptly."

It was so easy that it seemed too easy. Martin did not show any kind of serious fight, and it was hard to believe that he was one of Kohn's henchmen.

A few questions elicited the fact that Martin had been double-crossing his employer for several months, and that Kohn's interest in Renway had started in the July of that year. In that time Ritzy had slipped seven new cheques from Renway's current books, and later they had been forged and passed through safely. The total amount to date was about seven thousand pounds, with no individual cheque big enough to raise the bank's queries in an account of Renway's importance.

Interesting, though not vital, but it offered a theory.

Kohn was swindling the millionaire, without taking too much at a time, and meanwhile Irma was twisting the man round her little finger. The time would come when Kohn would make a really big haul, and Irma would persuade Renway to keep quiet.

But there was also the new business venture, which puzzled the Toff.

If Kohn was reckoning to cash in in a big way on the new venture, he was being a fool to take small amounts and risk the millionaire's reaction if it was discovered. The motives remained very vague, and the Toff had much to learn yet. But he was convinced that he had learned all he could from Ritzy.

He was deliberating on what to do with the man when he heard a car draw up outside.

The Toff, although he did not know it then, had made yet another error of judgment. And Ritzy, who knew this, had made a smaller one. He had shown the Toff into a room at the front of the house, where it was possible to hear the arrival of the car. On such small things depended the fortunes of the day.

For a split second the Toff saw the expression in Ritzy's eyes and he knew he had been tricked, or very close to it, knew why the man had raised so little protest. He did not let Ritzy see what he suspected, as he leaned back in his chair.

"Visitors?"

"I didn't expect them," said Ritzy quickly.

"Now they're here," said the Toff, "you'd better let them in."

"Sure, I ..." Ritzy jumped up.

"No, not so fast! I'm coming with you."

The man's face paled as the Toff put his hand to his pocket, where a gun bulged.

"I'm coming as far as this door," he said, "and I'll have you under my eye all the time. You get the idea? A false move from Ritzy and he earns a beautiful coffin. Get going."

Ritzy obeyed, but although the Toff knew he was on edge he was not sure that the man was really as scared as he made out.

The front door opened, and the Toff had a surprise.

Irma – *and* Kohn!

Irma was snuggled in furs which made her look even lovelier than ever, while Kohn was wearing a heavy coat with an astrakhan collar of immense proportions.

They could not see him, and the door closed on them.

Ritzy was one problem, Irma and Kohn together were quite another. It was a bad moment. The Toff was glad to remember that he had telephoned the Yard.

The thought was hardly in his mind, Irma and Kohn had not reached the door, nor seen him, when the cry came from upstairs. A woman's voice, high-pitched.

"Jim! Jim!"

The Toff went very still.

Kohn swore, Ritzy's face paled, although the Toff did not see it, and Irma's lips twisted.

"Keep that girl quiet, Martin!"

And then Irma saw the Toff, who had stepped out from his cover and whose automatic was now showing. He was smiling, and yet he looked a long way from being amused. For he had attacked, and thus precipitated a crisis, perhaps *the* crisis.

In the very house where Phyllis Bailey was a prisoner.

Chapter Sixteen

Fifty-Fifty

It was as bad a moment in its way for the Toff as it was for Irma and Kohn. He had come to see Ritzy, to forge the chain of evidence against Kohn, to build a case on which the police could act swiftly and without any doubt of a successful issue. He had enough to connect Kohn with Sidey's murder, for he believed he could force both Martin and Benson to testify once Kohn was under lock and key.

Kohn's arrival, with Irma's, had presented fresh difficulties, but none which were insuperable, however, so long as he had only himself to worry about.

It was very different now that he knew Wrightson's girl was upstairs, and in all probability Wrightson with her.

But he had the initial advantage, for both Irma and Kohn were startled by the sight of him, by the gun which he held so nonchalantly in his hand, and the smile which covered his true feelings.

The Toff broke the silence.

"Hallo," he said. "You've come just at the right moment, Leo, keep your hand away from your pocket. Irma, you can talk nicely now and tell me everything little Ritzy has forgotten. But first—*why* desert dear Paul today?"

Irma smiled.

The Toff gave her credit for having a nerve as cool as his own, although he saw the glitter in her eyes.

"How you do talk," she said. "Put that gun away, Rollison, and be sensible."

"I'm sorry," said the Toff. "Congenital inability prevents me. Ritzy, don't slink behind Leo—this really is a gun."

He was talking quickly, and he seemed absolutely in control of the situation, but all the time he was wondering how he was going to squeeze out of it and yet learn all there was to learn.

And how to get upstairs, free the girl, and get away. The big trouble was that there might be others in the house besides the three in front of him.

And then Ritzy gave him an opportunity he had not expected.

Ritzy's face was very pale, and Kohn's expression as he looked at the man was malevolent beyond words.

"So you've been talking."

"I haven't!" cried Ritzy. "I lied to him!"

On the 'him' he jumped forward. Perhaps because he wanted to prove to Kohn that he was no squealer; perhaps because his nerves let him down. In any case, he jumped, but before he had covered three feet the Toff's gun spoke. Ritzy uttered a cry as a bullet bit through his calf, and he dropped to the ground.

"Any more for the buggy ride?" asked the Toff.

Kohn raised his right foot and kicked Ritzy savagely on the side of the head. The crack echoed along the passage, and Ritzy uttered a single cry, and then went very still.

The expression in the Toff's eyes was hard.

"What a nice man you are, Leo. Get upstairs, both of you."

Neither moved.

The Toff forced an issue the best way he knew.

He fired again, and the bullet nicked Kohn's left leg. Kohn flinched, and his eyes blazed, but he stepped towards the stairs. Irma followed him, walking backwards so that her eyes were matching the Toff's all the time.

"Up," murmured the Toff, "or, if you prefer it, excelsior. So you invented the elopement as well as the new company, did you? Almost clever."

"Rollison ..."

"Let him talk," Kohn snapped. "He won't be able to for long."

"I've finished taking orders," snapped Irma, and the hostility between her and Kohn seemed about to flare up. "I've a proposition, Rollison."

"Propose as you climb, my pet."

"You're smart, but when you've got the girl and Wrightson you'll have them to look after as well as yourself. You'll have a handful, and you won't be able to get away."

"So the state of their health is as bad as that, is it?"

"They're temporarily out of action, and there are more of our men upstairs. But I'll give you a fifty-fifty chance."

They had reached the top of the stairs now and were standing on a small landing from which led two passages. The only light was from a dim yellow lamp, and there was no sound. One man might be there, or half a dozen – or none at all. The Toff was in no two minds about the possible danger, and he did not like the look of the situation which might develop. Kohn's manner was not that of a man afraid for his life.

"Fifty-fifty what?" said the Toff.

"You can take Wrightson and the girl," said Irma. "We won't stop you. But you'll keep out of this business from now until …"

Rollison shrugged.

"No deal, Irma."

"You're so impatient," said Irma, easily; "let me finish. Until tomorrow. Just for tonight."

The Toff confounded the gloom, for he could not see her expression. As it was, he had to judge from the inflection of her voice just why the suggestion was put forward. He imagined that she was worrying most about her own safety. Certainly it would be a big thing if he could get away with the girl and Wrightson.

"I might take you," he said, "up to midnight."

"That will do."

"Oh, no," said Kohn, and the Toff knew from the concentrated fury in his voice that he would gladly have strangled his accomplice. "Rollison's found his own way in; he can find his own way out."

"You'll change your mind," said Irma. She spoke under her breath, and the Toff didn't catch her words. Kohn did, and grunted. Irma said: "It's a deal, Rollison?"

"It's a deal," said the Toff, "as soon as the others are out in the street."

"I'll arrange it," said Irma.

In the darkness of the landing he could just see her as she moved. Kohn turned, too, but the Toff warned him to stay. A door opened softly, and Irma's voice came clearly: "Take her downstairs, Tike."

Who Tike was the Toff did not know; he did know the roughneck, who had certainly drunk Charlie Wray's beer, and who came out of the room carrying the girl over his shoulder, fireman fashion. He stopped for a moment when he saw the Toff.

"Hurry!" snapped Irma.

The Toff let the man pass, and heard him go down the stairs to return for Wrightson. The Toff recognised Wrightson's fair, crisp hair, as Tike half carried, half dragged him.

"There you are," Irma said. There was mockery and yet relief in her voice. "A truce until midnight, Rollison. I shall probably be in bad with Leo over this, but I'll risk it."

"Nice of you," said the Toff. "Can Tike drive a car?"

"He can."

"Tell him to go a hundred yards along the street and bring my Frazer-Nash," said the Toff. "He can put the youngsters in, and that will be enough for tonight."

There was a chance that someone would see what happened in the street unless things were done quickly; he grinned when Kohn helped the roughneck to load the car. Irma was standing near the Toff, who had pocketed his gun. It was an odd fact that he knew he could take Irma's word for it that she would not cause trouble – nor let anyone else cause it – until midnight. He was relieved up to a point.

There had been one reason only, of course, why he had taken the offer, and allowed them some three hours in which to work. Wrightson and the girl would have been in poor shape had he insisted on fighting, and even had Tike been the only other man in the house, the odds would have been heavy enough to make the situation ugly.

Irma, of course, had realised that in a shooting match she or Kohn, and perhaps both of them, would have been put out of action. She was thinking of herself; the undercurrent of enmity between her and Kohn was becoming more obvious with every encounter. But in her whisper to the man she had persuaded him to withdraw his objections to the bargain she had struck.

Odd that the Toff could trust her.

There were times when he was almost fond of Irma, others when he hated her, when he wanted nothing better than to see her in the dock.

She had wanted that margin of safety, and he had accepted for one good reason; but there was another thing which had been in his mind all the time. In three hours Irma and Kohn could do little. They had wanted breathing space, and the Toff could also do with it.

There was another factor; Wrightson and the girl were unimportant in their scheme, or Irma would not have let them go so easily.

"You were wrong," said Kohn coldly, "and you'll pay for it."

"I sometimes wonder," said Irma sharply, "whether you really are the fool you often look. What do you think Rollison is? You saw him shoot Ritzy, and he took the skin off your leg. If he'd wanted to force things then, he would have done. He needed time, and so did we."

"He should never have been allowed to go."

"But you might have been dead, and certainly you wouldn't have been able to walk. In any case, we haven't lost much. The mistake was in taking them."

Kohn shrugged his shoulders, and turned to a sideboard in the downstairs room. He served himself a drink, and raised it.

"All right, have it your own way. But we'll have to move fast, now, and we want Renway."

"Not for a few days," said Irma. "We do want to learn what Ritzy told the Toff – if you haven't killed him." Her tone was conciliatory; how that she had gained her point, she allowed her enmity to sink out of sight.

Kohn had not killed Ritzy, but that handsome man was unconscious and likely to be so for some time. They moved him from Abbott Road to a bide-out nearer Wapping, and Tike went with him. Kohn superintended the removal, while Irma took a taxi to St. John's Wood.

Renway was in, and his face brightened when he saw her.

"I didn't expect you tonight, my dear, but you're always welcome."

Irma laughed, and took a cigarette from her case.

"I felt fed-up, Paul. And I'm worried in case this thing doesn't go through."

Renway smiled. He looked younger, and moved more easily about the room.

"Nothing I back is a failure, Irma. The company is to be floated in two days, and the money will pour in. The directorate will do very well, I can assure you, very well indeed. A gin and Italian, my dear, or something stronger?"

"Gin and It, thanks," Irma said.

She felt tired. The affair at Abbott Road had taken a lot out of her, and the task of persuading Kohn had taken, more. But in two days the new company would be on the market, the shares subscribed. Within forty-eight hours of that, she and Kohn would have their rake-off.

It was so easy. Even the Toff would be able to do nothing to stop the getaway, for until the money was gone there was nothing illegal, everything was fair and above-board.

Afterwards, Renway would be the scapegoat. He would be accused of the swindle, and when his finances were examined they would be found in a chaotic state of disorder. With the help of Ritzy and Kohn, Irma had seen to that.

It was surprising how easy it was – while Kohn, by forcing the issue with Rollison that night, might have smashed the whole plot.

The other directors of the company were unimportant, and would never be directly involved. The verdict of the City would be that Renway had suffered heavily, and had resorted to a fraudulent promotion in an attempt to recoup his losses.

Of course, Renway must die – by natural causes; a slight overdose of the drug he took for his weak heart would be easy to administer, and there would be no trouble with the medical certificate.

She would be suspected, of course, if only because of Rollison; but there would be no proof. She and Kohn would cash in and disappear. He was not officially associated with Renway; no one would suspect him. Kohn had planned well, Irma had superintended most of the execution, and in a few days they would see results.

She thought of Renway again, without remorse, pleased that the boredom of his presence would soon be over. Renway raised his head.

"Something amusing you, my dear?"

"Odd thoughts," she said evasively. He could not see her expression, for she was bending over the fire. "I shall be glad when it's finished."

Renway leaned forward and patted her hand.

"Don't forget it's for you, Irma. For you and me."

She looked up, and in her eyes was a veiled promise, while her smile was sleepy and provocative.

"Of course," she said, "for you and me, Paul."

Ritzy had never particularly liked Leopold Kohn, and when he recovered consciousness his thoughts were vitriolic. He had little regard for the sanctity of human life, and he felt like murder.

He was very deep in this affair.

He was hoping to get a lot out of it, for the murder of Minnie Sidey had been cleverly managed. He had killed her because he realised Kohn was right when he had said the woman might squeal on Benson. He knew he was in Kohn's hands, knew now that while Kohn lived he would never be safe. He felt the ugly bruise where Kohn had kicked him, and before he left the Wapping house he put an automatic, fully loaded, in his pocket.

The Toff learned two things soon after he left Abbott Road. One of them gave him considerable satisfaction, and the other he found baffling.

Wrightson and the girl were not badly injured, and Wrightson was able to talk, even during the journey to the Toff's flat.

The girl was still under the influence of drugs, and Wrightson told the Toff that her cry had been uttered while unconscious. Wrightson had been in the room with her, tied hand and foot. The man Tike had been there, and had simply stepped across the room and struck her. In her near coma she had whimpered, and kept quiet.

But Wrightson did not know why he had been attacked. He could offer no explanation, even when they reached the flat. Soon the girl was in bed and resting, and Wrightson and the Toff were sitting opposite each other, strengthened by whiskies-and-sodas and cigarettes. Wrightson looked worn out.

"There must be a reason," said the Toff, "but it seems that they think you have served your purpose, or there would have been more trouble about letting you go. I suppose your uncle isn't aware of being swindled?"

Wrightson scowled.

"Not a chance."

"Somehow," said the Toff, "I can't associate Irma with the marry-then-murder idea. It has too many pitfalls, and it's not her idea of a game. After her own fashion, she's quite sporting."

"The Curtis woman—sporting!"

"Call her Cardew," said the Toff, with his lazy smile. "Yes, up to a point. I suppose, Wrightson, there's no possibility that the company's a rig-up, and that Renway knows it?"

Wrightson coloured.

"My uncle's honest if he's nothing else."

"Which is something," said the Toff.

Wrightson muttered uneasily, but the Toff left the subject and did not return to it. Wrightson had had more than enough, and the Toff persuaded him to go to bed.

When he had gone, the Toff sat back in his arm-chair, with his feet on the mantelpiece and looked at the clock. It wanted twenty minutes to twelve, and he was feeling impatient, half wishing he had made no bargain.

Jolly was back, with nothing to report.

Wrightson's confirmation that the new company was to be put on the market in a couple of days was the only information that seemed likely to offer results. Its shares would probably be well subscribed, and there was bound to be a great deal of money changing hands. That was what puzzled the Toff. It would merely go from one bank to another; there was no hard cash to handle, and no bullion.

Midnight struck.

At five minutes past the hour, he was ringing the bell at the St. John's Wood house. Late though it was, a footman opened the door, and in a few seconds Rollison was in the library, shaking hands with Renway.

Renway looked his surprise.

"My dear Rollison, an unexpected pleasure. What can I do for you so late at night?"

Rollison said: "I don't know that I've a pleasant job, but it's got to be done. About your nephew, Mr. Renway."

Renway's expression darkened.

"I'm not interested in my nephew."

"I think you will be."

"If you have come as a messenger from him …"

"I haven't," said the Toff. "I've come to tell you he didn't elope, Renway. He was struck over the head and kidnapped. So was Miss Bailey."

Renway half rose from his chair.

"James kidnapped! It's absurd!"

"But very true," said the Toff.

Renway stamped across the room, his hands clenched, his eyes glaring, his usually pallid face red with rage.

"It's outrageous! Prove it, Rollison, tell me what .you have to do with it, tell me who …"

"Steady," said the Toff. "He's safe and well, I can tell you that."

"Are you sure?"

"You can take my word for it."

"Then who arranged it?"

"You know the woman as Curtis, but her real name is Cardew. Obviously, she made it look like an elopement to prevent police inquiries. These are *facts*, Renway."

Paul Renway stared at him without speaking. His earlier sprightliness had dropped away, and it would have been easy to feel sorry for the man. The Toff would have done so, in some circumstances, but at the moment he was too full of his own thoughts.

"I—I can't believe this," Renway said hoarsely. "Irma, of all people. You'll have to offer me convincing proof, Rollison. *Very* convincing proof."

"I can. But first, Renway—how long had you known her before you realised she was Irma Cardew? Did you know it at first, or did you learn afterwards?"

Renway stiffened.

"Rollison, what are you suggesting?"

"That you haven't been so deceived as you would like to make out," said Rollison quietly. "Are you working with them, or entirely on your own? I fancy," added the Toff, "that you're on your own, and that you're making very pretty fools out of Irma and Kohn."

He stopped, for Renway's eyes showed naked hatred and the Toff knew he had found the truth.

Renway was in the new company ramp. *Renway* was not being fooled.

Chapter Seventeen

Quick Finish

Renway had one arm uplifted, and he took half a step forward. Then he staggered, and put his arm down to support himself against the table. His face, particularly at the lips and nose, had a bluish tinge.

"How—how did you learn?"

"The so-called elopement told me a great deal," said the Toff. "It was obvious, after I had made a few inquiries, that you would know there had been no elopement, yet you affected to believe the story. From then on, it was open and shut. Irma and Kohn had been using you as a dupe, as they thought, while you had them fooled."

Renway's lips worked.

"Rollison—Rollison, listen to me! I've been doing very badly. I'm insolvent. If I don't get through with this, I'll be broken. It will make hundres of thousands, and Irma and Kohn can take the blame. They don't know that I've been waiting for them, waiting for the money to come in, for the credits to be transferred to their accounts – accounts *I* can control. Before they put their hands on a penny I'll warn the police what they're going. It's a ramp, but they'll be blamed, no one will suspect me. I'll take you in as partner, Rollison! Keep your theories to yourself, that's all you have to do."

Rollison was silent for a moment.

He had realised that Renway was in it from the moment he had been sure of the kidnapping; but that Renway had been foxing so cleverly, planning to double-cross Irma and Kohn, had an irony that took his breath away.

Kohn was *not* so clever.

Nor was Irma.

"Well?" Renway snapped, "Will you do it?"

"Why did you let your nephew disappear and make no fuss?" asked the Toff.

"I thought he might guess something, and he was better out of the way for a while. The fool Kohn thought of it, of course; he didn't tell me, but I knew. He probably wanted to know what you'd been talking to Jim about. Rollison, it's absolutely foolproof, I tell you. Martin and Sidey worked for Kohn, and I can prove it. They're both in this; it looks as if Kohn planted them on me. I've even let them cash forged cheques to make the case against them all foolproof. It can't fail, Rollison, if you'll keep quiet."

"Can't it?" came a voice from the door.

It was then that the Toff was outplayed, that he knew he had lost himself too deeply in Renway's story to take heed of other possible threats. He half-turned, to see Irma in the doorway, still muffled in furs and still smiling – but not pleasantly. In her gloved hand was an automatic, while Kohn, standing just behind her, carried another.

Renway licked his lips, and seemed to shrink into himself.

Rollison kept his hands in sight; to go for his gun then would be to invite murder.

"Can't it fail?" asked Irma again, and she spoke very softly. "You've been clever, Paul, much cleverer than I thought; but it can fail all right."

Kohn pushed past her.

It was a foolish thing to do, and for a split second Rollison considered going for his gun. He decided against it; while Kohn reached Renway and hit him. It was a blow of the kind he had delivered against Phyllis Bailey, on a par with the kicking of Ritzy. It showed that his temper was ungovernable, and that just then he was in the white heat of rage; his eyes were glaring and red-rimmed, as if he had no self-control.

Renway fell across the desk.

"No, don't, don't …"

"I'll break your bloody neck," snarled Kohn. "You'd put this across me, would you? I …"

He raised his clenched fist again, but Irma's cold voice cut across his words, making him hesitate.

"Don't be a fool all the time, Leo; that won't do any good. We're through, and we've got to get our hands on what money we can. Get his keys."

"A nice thought," said the Toff, and his voice was amiable. "I wish I could think you were just being kind-hearted, Irma."

"That's enough from you," said Irma. "You didn't lose much time working."

"I started on the stroke of twelve," said the Toff, and he selected a cigarette from the table. Kohn was going through Renway's pockets for his keys. He found them, and stepped to the safe behind the desk. As he opened the safe, the Toff struck a match to light his cigarette. Irma watched him closely, knowing that what danger there was would come from Rollison, and wondering whether she would get away in time.

Kohn was taking bundles of notes out of the safe.

The Toff saw them, and knew that Renway had been preparing against the failure of his coup, for there were several thousands of pounds there, all in small wads of banknotes. Kohn stuffed them into his pocket, and turned to Irma.

"That's the lot."

"Yes," said Irma, and she laughed. "Renway, you poor fool, you're going out."

She fired towards the man.

Renway reared up, and then slumped down. The bullet went well above his head, and the Toff thought that she had intended to fire high; but he doubted whether a bullet through the heart would have been of more effect, for there was an ominous rattle in the old man's throat. He himself was stiff with tension, for he expected the next bullet to come his way.

"Going out of black?" he asked, and there was a challenge in his voice.

"Yes," said Irma. "But for some reason I don't want to kill you, Rollison. You've played by the rules, and ..."

Kohn snapped: "Put him out, now!"

"Leo, this is my game. I ..."

Kohn swore, and fired from his pocket. He sent Irma's gun flying from her hand, and he swung round on the Toff, beside him. A split second more, and the Toff could have won; but as it was he saw only murder in Kohn's hands.

And then:

Crack!

The first shot had been barely audible, for Kohn's gun was fitted with a silencer. The second was loud and clear, and did not come from Kohn. It came from the door, and the bullet hit Kohn in the chest. A second followed, and a hole leapt into his temple. He lurched forward, dead before he touched the ground, while in the doorway stood Ritzy Martin. Ritzy's lips were twisted; a heavy revolver was smoking in his hand.

"That's one of you," he sneered. "Now you, Irma ..."

And then the Toff fired.

Ritzy reared up, a strained surprised expression on his handsome face. His gun dropped, and did not fire again. For a few seconds it was like a tableau, with Irma standing and nursing one wrist, Kohn and Renway dead on the floor, and Ritzy Martin dying. He tried to speak, but he failed, his big body slumping heavily.

The Toff's eyes met Irma's.

They were silent for a moment, with her entirely at his mercy. And then he said, in a voice which she hardly recognised: "Make it, my pet. Don't waste any time in getting out of London. I'm sending for McNab at once. He'll pull in Wray and Benson, and you'll be lucky to get out of England before they've talked."

Irma said: "Thanks, Rollison. Is there anything you want to know?"

"Did Minnie know about the job?"

"Yes; Kohn paid her five hundred to keep silent."

"Was Wrightson involved?"

"No."

"Why *was* he kidnapped?"

"Because he would make a nuisance of himself after his girl had gone. Kohn wanted her, to find out what you'd said to Wrightson."

"Involved," said Rollison. "Kohn seemed so simple, too, but he made too many mistakes. All right, Irma. But remember, there's no next time. Not this way."

"I'll remember," she said.

She half-turned, as the Toff called: "What money have you got?"

"A few hundred pound, but not with me."

"Take some from Kohn; no one will miss it."

There was a twisted smile on her lips as she took two of the bundles that Kohn had taken from the safe. She looked at Rollison once, and then quickly away.

He waited until she had left the room before he stepped to the telephone. While he was asking for McNab, a scared voice came from the door. A footman was standing there, holding a poker.

"Is—is anything the matter?"

"Sleeping sickness," said the Toff abruptly. "Get upstairs and stay there."

The man disappeared, while the Toff lit a cigarette and then stepped to Renway. The man was dead, as were the others.

The affair was over, and to him it seemed that this was the best way. The Sideys had been avenged; only Charlie Wray was free, and he would not be so for long. Irma had a sporting chance of a getaway, and he felt that she had earned it.

He did not tell McNab that, and he kept Irma's name out of things until the early hours of the morning, after McNab had taken the rest of his story, interviewed Benson, and arrested Charlie Wray.

McNab was on top of the world, for he had solved his case, and even had a victim for trial. The hard words which had been said of him by the Assistant Commissioner would be withdrawn, and McNab's honesty compelled him to admit that it was due only to the Toff.

"Why didn't you mention Irma Cardew earlier, Rollison?"

"I forgot," said the Toff, very gently. "She was trying to marry Renway, so she would hardly have wanted him dead."

McNab grunted, and composed further questions for Benson and Wray. Within an hour, the call was out for Irma, and the Toff marvelled at himself for hoping that she would get away in time. It transpired that she had caught a night tourist plane. The Toff did not think she would land in McNab's net, once in Paris.

He felt pleased with life.

So did Wrightson and his Phyllis, despite the scandal.

So did Anthea, when the Toff went along to see her, and gave her the outlines of the story. She was in bed again, for her visit to him had damaged her ankle more than had at first been thought, but she was not complaining.

At her bedside were the five books which Phyllis Bailey had written.

"I'm enjoying them," said Anthea. "Have a chocolate?"

"Thanks," said Rollison. He ate one reflectively, eyeing her with amusement. "You certainly take things as they come, my dear, and you don't realise that you played a bigger part in this than you wot of. I doubt whether I could have forced the issue without you."

"Good," said Anthea enthusiastically. "I was worried almost grey, Rolly, but since I've known it's over, I've decided that you have so much luck that you're not worth worrying about. Jamie may be a bit dull and staid, but I rather like a quiet life."

"Go to it," said the Toff.

He turned to leave her, but she held his hand, pulled him down towards her, and kissed him. It was a gentle kiss, and her eyes were gleaming as she let him go.

"That's a kind of kiss I can teach you, Rolly."

"Learned from Jamie?" asked the Toff. "Be advised, my sweet, it's the best kind. Do you mind if I go?"

"Will you look me up from time to time?"

"I will, when you're safely married, and no longer a temptation."

"I think", said Anthea quietly and seriously, "that that's the nicest compliment I've had, Rolly. Goodbye, for now, and good luck. And be careful."

"As always," said the Toff.

He walked back to his flat thoughtfully, thinking a great deal about Anthea.

Long before he reached Gresham Terrace, however, his mind had turned to Irma. He wondered soberly where she was, if he had seen the last of her, and whether he would live to regret the fact that he had let her go. She had saved his life, and she had played according to the rules of their queer game.

In her own way.

The Toff shrugged, and let himself into his flat. It was pleasant not to have to take precautions as he went in, pleasant to see Jolly framed in the kitchen door, looking gloomy and eyeing a hob-nailed boot with some disfavour.

"May this be thrown away, sir?"

"It may not," said Rollison firmly, and he glanced towards that wall which was covered with souvenirs. "Find a place of honour for it, Jolly, and dust it zealously every day."

"As you say, sir," said Jolly, resignedly.

"And another thing," said the Toff. "You will recall a wager on the subject of Kohn—his cleverness as against his mistakes?"

"I do, sir."

"Then remember that you owe me half a crown," said the Toff.

"I beg leave to differ, sir," said Jolly. "I placed the coin on your dressing-table just before you came in."

John Creasey

Gideon's Day

Gideon's day is a busy one. He balances family commitments with solving a series of seemingly unrelated crimes from which a plot nonetheless evolves and a mystery is solved.

One of the most senior officers within Scotland Yard, George Gideon's crime solving abilities are in the finest traditions of London's world famous police headquarters. His analytical brain and sense of fairness is respected by colleagues and villains alike.

'The finest of all Scotland Yard series' – New York Times.

Gideon's Fire

Commander George Gideon of Scotland Yard has to deal successively with news of a mass murderer, a depraved maniac, and the deaths of a family in an arson attack on an old building south of the river. This leaves little time for the crisis developing at home ....

'Gideon of Scotland Yard emerges as one of the most real working detectives in modern fiction.... A sympathetic and believable professional policeman.' - New York Times

JOHN CREASEY

THE CREEPERS

"The prisoner's hand was thin and bony ... And in the centre of the palm was a pinkish mark. It was the shape of a wolf's head, mouth open, fangs showing. Although it was what he had expected to see, Inspector West felt a twinge of repugnance a stab not unrelated to fear. It was the fifth time he had seen the mark of the wolf – the mark of Lobo."

A gang of cat burglars led by Lobo cause mayhem as they terrorize the city. They must be stopped, but with little in the way of evidence the police are baffled. Just how can Inspector West manage to do this in what is a race against time before more victims succumb?

"Here is an excellent novel of law enforcement officers, harried, discouraged and desperately fatigued, moving inexorably ahead under the pressure of knowledge that they must succeed to save human lives." - Cleveland Plain-Dealer

"Furiously exciting" - Chicago Tribune

"The action is fast, continuous and exciting" - San Francisco News

John Creasey

Introducing the Toff

Whilst returning home from a cricket match at his father's country home, the Honourable Richard Rollison - alias The Toff - comes across an accident which proves to be a mystery. As he delves deeper into the matter with his usual perseverance and thoroughness , murder and suspense form the backdrop to a fast moving and exciting adventure.

'The Toff has been promoted to a place of honour among amateur detectives.' – The Times Literary Supplement

Case Against Paul Raeburn

Chief Inspector Roger West has been watching and waiting for over two years – he is determined to catch Paul Raeburn out. The millionaire racketeer may have made a mistake, following the killing of a small time crook.

Can the ace detective triumph over the evil Raeburn in what are very difficult circumstances? This cannot be assumed as not eveything, it would seem, is as simple as it first appears .....

'Creasey can drive a narrative along like nobody's business ... ingenious plot ... interesting background .' - The Sunday Times